T0147496

THE TWINNING
VERSE THREE

THE TWINNING
VERSE THREE

The Song of the Seraphim

Justin R. Cary

iUniverse, Inc.
Bloomington

The Twinning Verse Three
The Song of the Seraphim

iUniverse books may be ordered through booksellers or by contacting:

iUniverse
1663 Liberty Drive
Bloomington, IN 47403
www.iuniverse.com
1-800-Authors (1-800-288-4677)

ISBN: 978-1-4759-5437-1 (sc)
ISBN: 978-1-4759-5438-8 (ebk)

Printed in the United States of America

iUniverse rev. date: 10/03/2012

CONTENTS

Chapter 1   The Woman in the Desert.......................... 3
Chapter 2   The Queen, Once Upon a Time 12
Chapter 3   In a Mirror, Darkly 23
Chapter 4   Secret Stories... 30
Chapter 5   Footsteps in the Snow 43
Chapter 6   The Cold, Grey North 55
Chapter 7   An Empty Stall... 60
Chapter 8   Echoes of the Past 65
Chapter 9   Memories in the Snow 68
Chapter 10   The Dark Caress of Dreams 73

Part 2

Chapter 1   Cyril 93
Chapter 2   Encounter in the Woods 96
Chapter 3   Chamber of the Seraphim 105
Chapter 4   In the White Loam 110
Chapter 5   The Truth at Last 114
Chapter 6   Lillian's Goodbye.................................. 130
Chapter 7   Clouds on the Horizon 137
Chapter 8   A Gift From Long Ago.......................... 139
Chapter 9   Treasure Island 145
Chapter 10   Return to Castle Blanchfield 148
Chapter 11   A Dark Reunion.................................... 150
Chapter 12   The Book.. 154

Chapter 13   Back to the Bathroom 159
Chapter 14   Carried Away 168
Chapter 15   Twilight Creatures................................. 174
Chapter 16   It Begins.. 179
Chapter 17   The Razing of Aside.............................. 183
Chapter 18   In Couplet Canyon Once More 190
Chapter 19   Dunny and Quixitix 193
Chapter 20   In The Twinning................................... 197
Chapter 21   Cyril's Gift 203
Chapter 22   Another Compass 209
Chapter 23   Voices From Beyond 212
Chapter 24   Together Again...................................... 217
Chapter 25   Ja'Mirra.. 221
Chapter 26   Allcraft's Plan 226
Chapter 27   Michael Smith 232
Chapter 28   Mya's Journey....................................... 237
Chapter 29   The Departure 243
Chapter 30   The Song of the Seraphim.................... 246

Epilogue.. 253
Author's Note.. 257

For my parents.

Always loving

Always giving

Always inspiring

For my partner Erica.
You are love, grace, respect and everything I cherish in this world.

<u>Weave In</u>

Weave in, weave in, my hardy life,
Weave yet a soldier strong and full for great campaigns to come,
Weave in red blood, weave sinews in like ropes, the senses, sight weave in,
Weave lasting sure, weave day and night the wet, the warp, incessant weave, tire not,
(We know not what the use O life, nor know the aim, the end, nor really aught we know,
But know the work, the need goes on and shall go on, the death-envelop'd march of peace as well as war goes on,)
For great campaigns of peace the same the wiry threads to weave,
We know not why or what, yet weave, forever weave.

-Walt Whitman, *Leaves of Grass*

<u>Design</u>

I found a dimpled sider, fat and white,
On a white heal-all, holding up a moth
Like a white piece of rigid satin cloth—
Assorted characters of death and blight
Mixed ready to begin the morning right,
Like the ingredients of a witches' broth—
A snow-drop spider, a flower like a froth,
And dead wings carried like a paper kite.

What had that flower to do with being white,
The wayside blue and innocent heal-all?
What brought the kindred spider to that height,
Then steered the white moth thither in the night?
What but design of darkness to appall?—
If design govern a thing so small.

-Robert Frost

The Madison Times-Dispatch

Local Retirement Community Abandoned

Susan Berkly, staff writer

Friends, family members and nearly everyone else in York County awoke Sunday morning to a bizarre situation; every resident of the Brandywine Retirement Home missing without a trace.

"It's like they just vanished." Sergeant Steven Ashford spoke with reporters on the scene Sunday morning to a back drop of swirling red and blue sirens, yellow police tape, and concerned family members looking on. "At this point we have no leads. If these people were kidnapped, I'm not sure how it could have happened. I mean, we're talking about TVs left on, water left running, stoves burning . . . it really is like they just disappeared," said Ashford.

Brandywine Retirement Home, established in 1984, has become the most prestigious and expensive retirement community in Wisconsin with people retiring here from all over the state.

"Maybe somebody took them for money," said Abigail Winston, 16. Her grandmother, Charlotte Winston, is one of the missing residents. "I don't care what it was, I just want my Nanna back."

Residents of York County and the police force are both baffled. The police claim to have not received any kind of ransom note or other form of communication from a possible kidnapper and the people of York County have been left with nothing but more questions.

"Her bed wasn't made. My mother would never leave her bed unmade," said Gretchen Wily, 47. "I grew up with her and spent everyday of my childhood with her. She made that bed every morning, first thing, before she even put her slippers on; made me make mine too. When we went to her room I cried when I saw it . . . her bed wasn't made . . . what happened to our loved ones here?"

The answer to that question remains unanswered although police and local authorities have assured residents their relatives and loved ones will be found soon.

CHAPTER 1

▼

THE WOMAN IN THE DESERT

As the final rays of light, carried to Serafina upon a slowly descending sun, skirted over the horizon and cast one last, longing look upon the dried valley, the woman felt the first chill wind of evening sweep over her body. She had spent seven long days and six nights in this particular valley; eating what she could find, drinking what little water she had brought with her (sometimes Fabricating more), sleeping only when she needed it and only for short intervals. This night would be the seventh and the last. She would have to return tomorrow and if she found nothing tonight then she would return empty handed. She pulled the brown and tattered hood of her long cloak tighter around her dirty blond hair and continued moving.

As she walked she listened to the sandy wind sweep through the valley, scratching over the hardpan and crabgrass. Although her father had told her many stories of the desolate deserts of Sardorchester, she never actually thought she would see them for herself. The wind sounded like music from a flute at times, whistling through the crags and boulders on the horizon, and at other times it sounded like a witch's cackle; hollow and desperate. To the east, a coyote or craghound howled but the woman paid no attention to the sound. She had seen far, far worse than coyotes on her journey. Her journey . . . it seemed so long ago when she was only a child. How had things become so complicated so fast? Life was much different for her now, but she decided to spend no time with thoughts like those. Thoughts like those will drive a person crazy in the wild. Instead, she focused on her mother.

"I will be back in time," she whispered to herself. The wind caught her words and swirled them, tornado like, around her head and she could almost hear them echoing back to her. "I will see her again." She continued walking.

Later, the moon at her back and silence blanketing the caked and cracking hardpan below her, the woman came at last to what she was searching for. She stared for several minutes at her destination and let out a heavy and long sigh. The ground was rough and trodden; clearly a company had been here. She could see vague footprints in the moonlight leading to a small cave entrance in the side of the mountain. Like before, Quixitix had led her to the correct destination; his science accurate as always, but not fast enough.

"The same as the others . . . too late again," she said to no one.

Pulling the hood from her cloak tighter around her hair, the woman felt the long, tight braid beat upon her back as the wind picked it up. Her hair, long and messy, seemed to struggle against the braid which bound it. She longed for the days when she could afford the luxury of a proper hair cut or a long, relaxing bath . . . perhaps some music. She pushed these thoughts away as well. She had come here to find them . . . her mind doing its best work to push away the thought that she would find nothing yet again.

The structure stretching up toward the inky black sky greeted the woman with a smile full of rusted iron and baricite, copper, alumin and urah. Precious metals, long forgotten, the woman had only read about these in history books, stories of a world long past, a world of engines and steam, of metal and elaborate machinery ; the ancient days of Serafina. She found it hard to believe her world and that one were one in the same. Things were so different now; she wondered what it would have been like to grow up with little metal and iron toys, steam powered coaches and who knows what else. She allowed her mind a few moments to imagine a time before the Twinning; a time before the Order of the Fabricantresses, a time before war and turmoil and strife. Serafina had been much different then, according to myth and legend, before men and women began to draw from the Twinning and leave behind the ways of science and machines. Her own memories brought her away from her imaginings.

The woman thought of her toy horses and soldiers; she longed for those things now, longed for any vestiges of that life, the life she once had, the life she enjoyed before fate thrust all of this upon her . . . she pushed these thoughts away.

She closed her eyes for a moment and concentrated on the sound of the wind, the sound of the valley closing in and expanding all around her, the sound of the tiny fissures and cracks of the structure before her bending and breaking in thousands of microscopic, harmonious symphonies. Opening her eyes, she pulled a small rod from her pack. It was long and grey, extendable, and, flicking her wrist, the rod grew into a small staff. She whispered a word, very softly, and the end of the staff grew bright, illuminated. The light caused the building to appear even more freakish than before in the pale and haunting moonlight. The woman approached the maw as the coarse desert winds swirled and buffeted around her. Moments later she was inside, safe from the storm and standing in a small opening at the base of the structure. She paused for a moment and caught her breath, listening to the sand skirt across the cold metal of the building around her. Her staff brightened the entry way enough for her to see a few feet ahead. The floor, littered with various pieces of debris and chunks of rock or minerals, greeted her with little compassion. Her eyes caught something skitter across the dark floor but the shadow was gone before she had time to turn her head. The only sound was the low whistle of the sandstorm in the night. Shaking off the powder from her tunic, she unlatched the hood piece and felt it fall down around her shoulders.

The woman's dirty blond hair surged free as she shook her head in the small expanse of the entry way. Longer now and hard from days of travel, the woman's hair still emitted a particular sheen and shimmer, like the glow of a distant star. She stretched her back, her muscles pockets of tight and aching pain, and heard a few popping noises as she released the stored calcium in her bones. Her eyes brilliantly contrasted the dark passageway before her and the light from her staff tried to find its way down the velvet tunnel of darkness.

"Hello?" she called, her voice echoing off the metallic walls and rising above the sound of the wind outside. "Is anyone here?" she called again.

No response. She waited a few more moments; waiting, perhaps for a response or perhaps for someone to come and tell her she didn't have to go this time, she didn't have to find yet another abandoned site, yet another remnant of something long gone, something she felt she would never catch. She sighed in the darkness.

"Bright light," she spoke, her voice taking on the resonance and power of The Word. Her staff immediately grew brighter, the tip at the end now a fluorescent torch leading her forward. The hallway remained just as long as before and she could see no end, even with her newly illuminated torch. She moved forward.

Stepping slowly, the woman put one foot ahead of the next, taking extra care to avoid the scattered scraps on the floor. Her boots made loud clanging sounds on the metallic floor panels as she walked and she did her best to silence the noise. As she moved further into the darkness, she almost didn't notice it but little escaped her perception these days. The shadows around her had shifted, moved; just slightly. A normal observer would have remained oblivious but this particular woman had faced far worse than whatever was about to come at her from the belly of the dark tunnel. She knew one thing for certain; she had only moments to react. When she spoke, she barely vocalized the sounds. She barely even needed to whisper these days.

"Shield," she said. As though flowing out of her throat the words oozed down her neck and onto her shoulder, flowing along her arm until they formed a massive wooden shield around her wrist. Red and gold, the oval shield caught the light of the woman's staff and gleamed in the darkness, ready for anything. She felt something rush past on her right, something extremely fast. She stood motionless, focused on the darkness before her. Again, that rush, just past her head. She raised the shield slightly and as she did, she was knocked back with such force that she was lifted into the air and thrown nearly out of the entrance. Her wrist reverberated and cracked as the shield was hit with the mysterious, fast moving objects. She let out a small scream, mostly because she was startled; she had grown quite accustomed to pain, and landed hard on her back. Scrambling to get to her feet, she barely had time to stand when another object smashed into her shield. She heard the wood fibers crack and splinter with this second blow and she knew her shield would not take too many more.

"Enough of this," she said. Speaking a few quick words, the tunnel suddenly filled with light. As the light shot down the length of the tunnel like a wave, a massive wall followed behind it, moving and growing with every inch. The woman could hear the projectiles ricocheting and breaking upon the wall as it raced down the tunnel, blocking anything else with ease. At last the woman heard a massive crash and the wall stopped. She waited, listened, and watched. Nothing. Whatever had attacked her had been crushed by the newly Fabricated wall. Retracting her staff, the woman dropped the red and gold shield. She saw two massive spears sticking into the thick wood, long and black, with huge silver spearheads. As soon as the shield hit the floor it evaporated, leaving only the spears, which hit the ground and clanged against the metallic floor. The tunnel was now fully illuminated and the woman could see how far down it went.

"Not so bad," she said to herself. Placing her staff back into her bag, she proceeded. When she reached the extremity of the niche, she saw her wall and noticed a few tendrils of smoke snaking around from behind. Placing her hands on the wall, the structure evaporated as well, revealing the odd machination that had attacked her.

"Some kind of security device I suppose," she said. "Haven't seen one like this yet. I guess the architect liked spears." The device was elegant and simple; several long pipes protruded from the wall, each just slightly bigger than the spears that had been shot down the hallway. Now, most of them were flattened or crushed, a few had retracted back into the wall and, from the holes they had previously occupied, issued the smoke the woman had seen. "Clever."

Looking around, she noticed a small doorway, not much larger than her own body, to the left. She again muttered a few words and this passage way illuminated as well.

"After you," she said to no one. Then, to herself, "no, I insist, after you." She entered the doorway and soon found herself in a much larger room. Stone edifices and half-crumbling statues lined the walls, creatures and beings the woman had never seen before; except, of course, in rooms just like this one. Her footsteps made little noise on the hard stone as she made her way through the chamber, breathing in shallow, quick intakes of air. The air itself smelled acrid and filled with decay, but recent and fresh at the same time. Someone had been here. The light flowing from the woman's staff raced up and down the floor and walls of the chamber like sheets of wax casting an eerie glow upon the objects it touched. A sound, quick and quiet. The woman stood motionless, breath held, listening.

Again, a sound. Something trying to hide. With senses heightened and nerves extending like invisible fingers, the woman scanned the room trying to find the source of the noise. She saw nothing. Then she heard it again, higher this time. She looked up to see a few specs of stone falling from the head of a massive statue; something that looked like a cross between a bird and a woman. The shadows seemed to move and flow around the statue.

"Show yourself!" she exclaimed. She could hear the distress and near panic in her voice. "I won't ask again!" She received no reply from the murky shadows. The air suddenly grew very still and a voice, a voice like a sleepy snake, issued from the darkness around her.

"You . . . you . . . must leave . . . thiiisssss place."

"I will not," commanded the woman. "Where have they gone? Where is my brother?"

"You will . . . never see him . . . . again."

"Who are you?" she demanded.

"A warning . . ." Hissed the inky voice.

"What does that mean?"

"Abandon your quest . . . ."

"That, I cannot do."

"Then I cannot help you . . ."

Suddenly the shadows above the statue writhed violently, shook, and the woman watched as the statue's head cracked and began to tumble from its body. She had only moments to react; without a quick and instant evasive maneuver she would surely be crushed by the falling debris. She jumped, pumping with her legs and feet to achieve maximum distance, and as she left the ground the staff slipped from her hand sending shimmers of light in strange and skewed angles. The head fell and smashed into the floor, pieces of rock and stone spiraling everywhere, decimating the space the woman had moments before occupied. She landed a few feet away on something hard and metallic. She felt the object dig into her side and she let out a whine of pain.

"You will never reclaim him . . . . Mya VanVargott." The voice echoed around her and then the air returned to normal and the shadow was gone.

"I will." Her voice, stone cold, echoed in the empty chamber.

Wincing, she rose, nursing her side. She felt for blood but luckily there was none. Cautiously, Mya found her way to her staff, retrieved it, and walked back to see what she had landed on. The object was very strange but she had seen many like it before.

She picked it up and ran her fingers over it; a mask of some kind, made of dark copper, red and rusty. Two large holes for eyes to see through and an even larger hole which allowed space for a mouth; the mask was grotesque. An empty cavity adorned the forehead; something had been lodged there, something small and oval shaped. This mask was in much better shape than any of the ones Mya had encountered before and now she noticed something new; a device of some kind, hanging from the bottom of the mask by tendril-like wires, connected to a small box. Mya also noticed straps around the back of the mask; used to secure the thing to someone's head, she guessed.

"Just another empty shell," she said, dropping the metal faceplate. It landed on the rocks with a loud clang. Mya looked down, and sighed. Her long, dirty blonde hair hung around her body like a curtain. "Michael . . . ." She said to the darkness.

A quick examination of the rest of the room revealed little Mya had not seen before. A chair of some kind, decayed and broken, covered in rust, a few instruments, strange edifices and ancient, decaying stone. They were all the same.

"Michael . . ." she said. "Where are you?"

Mya made her way back to the entrance of the building. She listened to the desert prowling outside, a villain of sand and wind. She fastened the cloth around her face, stowed her staff, and proceeded into the swirling storm. The search would continue.

▼

CHAPTER 2

THE QUEEN,
ONCE UPON A TIME

"Anything?" The woman's frail and weak voice, echoless, fell flat in the quiet room. Outside the ocean waves lapped and danced upon the shore, their distant sound soft and comforting, floating through the air and into the room. The double doors of the terrace branched inward, open wide, and the sea breeze caused the gossamer curtains to billow in and out like silken lungs. The room was comfortable, easy, light; and that was exactly the way Mya wanted it. Mya sat, still and quite, next to her mother. Lillian lay upon a massive bed; pillows and blankets spread all around here, her body sinking into the soft mattress. Mya had returned from the desert of Sardorchester only hours ago and this had been her first stop.

"Nothing mother. I'm sorry," Mya said, holding Lillian's pale white hand. Lillian tried to strengthen her grip but produced only a weak squeeze. Mya barely felt it.

"How many is this now?" asked Lillian.

"I've lost count. Fifty maybe," replied Mya. Lillian tried to smile and Mya noticed the look of despair and fleeting hope flash across her eyes. The white bandages across her face and head made Lillian's porcelain skin look all the more alabaster. Mya watched as her mother's chest rose and fell with each shallow and difficult breath she took.

"How are you feeling today?" asked Mya.

"I'm fine dear," said Lillian, her lips parting briefly to expose the smallest of smiles. Mya smiled back and patted her mother's hand.

"Are they taking good care of you?"

"Yes, yes. The twins came by the other day," said Lillian, her eyes moving down to the floor.

"How do they seem?" asked Mya.

"They have grown so much . . . but their eyes . . . their eyes are just . . ."

"Empty," finished Mya. Lillian nodded. The salt air breathed through the window and Lillian closed her eyes and inhaled deeply.

"I love the sea," she said.

"I know mother," said Mya.

"You are so much older now Mya," said Lillian. Raising her hand very slowly, Lillian touched the side of Mya's face, her fingers moving up and down her daughter's smooth skin. The touch warmed Mya and comforted her. She struggled against thoughts that one day soon she would no longer be able to feel that caress.

"Lucious told me something strange," said Lillian, her eyes turning toward the blue and green water nestling closer and closer to the shoreline outside.

"Did he?"

"He has these dreams . . . he is a troubled child," said Lillian. She began to cough, harder and harder, her face going from white to red.

"Here mother," Mya said, pouring some water into a glass and handing it to her mother. Eventually the coughing subsided and Lillian took the glass, drinking slowly, barely holding herself up in the bed.

"Thank you," she said.

"Lucious' dreams?" asked Mya.

"Yes, strange and vivid dreams . . . and the way he describes them . . . frightening. I think that boy is very special Mya."

"I'm sure you're right."

Several moments passed by with only the soft sounds of the ocean filling the room. Sunlight seeped through the windows at slanted angles and Mya watched the dust fill the usually invisible light.

"You miss him Mya." It was not a question.

"Yes, everyday. Why did he go with Allcraft?" Mya's face looked hard and worn, the face of a woman living with betrayal and sorrow every day.

"That is something I ask myself each minute. I'm sure he had his reasons."

"Selfish reasons," said Mya. "To leave us all like this, to leave you like this . . ."

"It's alright child," said Lillian, patting Mya's hand. "He will come back to us, in time."

Mya did not respond. Instead, she smiled at her mother and Lillian smiled back.

"Let's talk of other things mother," said Mya. Lillian nodded.

"How are things out there?" asked Lillian, nodding her head toward the window.

"Not good. Once word spread that Allcraft the Magican has returned, people started getting scared, fleeing, abandoning everything. Blanchfield is . . ." Mya did not finish the sentence.

"It has been hard these past few years. The world is being torn apart Mya and all because of this one man. I hope you understand . . . what we had to do so long ago."

"Of course I do mother."

The sound of the marble door sliding open interrupted the women's talk. They turned to see their visitor.

"Hope 'oim not 'terrupting."

"Never Dunny, please come it."

It had been months since Mya last laid eyes on Dunmire Quixitix and those few months had not been kind to the massive, hulking figure before her. In fact, she could hardly classify him as massive and hulking anymore. He had lost weight, lost his usual insatiable desire for the taste of fine foods, since that day at the school . . . on the bridge. Mya pushed those thoughts away. She had promised herself at the ceremony she would leave such sorrows in the past.

"Brought you this ma'lady," said Dunny, placing a hand-picked bouquet of wild flowers on the table next to Lillian's bed; the beautiful Lilies and Towerdragon flowers bursting with life and color. The purple and blue flowers immediately saturated the air around them and Mya could smell the deep aroma of open fields and summer days.

"They're beautiful Dunmire, thank you."

"Course," said Dunny. "How are you feeling?"

"I'm alright," Lillian said. Mya could see that her mother did not believe the words.

"And you Mya? Glad to see you are back. Any luck this time? Did you find Michael?"

"No Dunny, I'm sorry. Just another desecrated tomb, the same as always. What are they doing there anyway? I'm sick of not knowing what it is I'm chasing."

Mya noticed Dunny's eyes slant toward the ground and his expression changed slightly, as though he was holding something back.

"What is it Dunny?"

Looking up at Mya, Dunny glanced around the room, still unwilling to breech the subject currently occupying his mind.

"It's hard 'ta talk about," said Dunny. "The Departure . . . Peter's departure. I've been having these dreams . . ."

Lillian stared at Dunny, intently listening to what he said.

"Go on," said Mya.

"Well, the dreams are so odd. We are all there, at the cliff . . . and then everyone is gone and it's just me, standin' alone. And there's this shadow . . ." He stopped, unsure how to continue. "It's hard ta' remember."

"It's alright Dunny . . ." said Mya, unsure what to do. She thought for a moment about revealing her dreams lately, but decided to refrain. "Just dreams Dunny."

"Maybe they mean somethin' Mya, maybe they are a clue to what's goin' on." Mya watched as Dunny's level of agitation rose.

"It's fine Dunny. Just dreams. Everything will be . . ." Mya's speech was cut off by the sound of Lillian coughing hard, rasping and rough.

"I understand," replied Dunny. "I should be goin'." Lillian continued to cough and Mya placed a handkerchief at her lips to catch the blood.

Dunny stood and bowed. Lillian's coughing began to subside. "Thankee both. I'll see ya' later." Leaving the room Dunny looked back once to see Mya, eyes to the floor, folding the bloody handkerchief, dirty blond hair scattered around her shoulders, so much longer now. The sound of the door closing punctuated the silence in the room, encroaching after the harsh sounds of Lillian's cough.

"I feel like I'm chasing my own tail mother. How do I even know this is the right path?"

"It is Mya, I can feel it. You are getting closer and you have been these past months. Every time you find one of those chambers you are one step closer to finding your brother, and Allcraft."

"But what are they? What are those strange masks and chairs? And this last time . . . have you any idea what that . . . that voice thing was?"

"I don't know Mya. Perhaps some creation from Allcraft's warped mind. Mya . . . have you been having dreams about Peter's Departure as well?"

Mya hesitated, deciding how to answer this question. Her dreams had been extremely vivid since that day; shadows, figures, people falling, dark skies and clouds . . . and the message.

"Yes . . ." she said.

"I thought you might. Can you tell me about them?"

"They all start the same. It's like a warning, a message. Telling me about the Chambers but not what they are, just that I have to find them to find Michael. Sometimes it's in the sky, sometimes in the trees. This sounds crazy, it's hard to describe."

"What else do you see?" asked Lillian.

"A figure; always in shadow. I don't know who he is; it's like dark clouds swirl around him at all times. It's like he wants to talk to me but I can't hear him."

"I see," said Lillian.

"And always I'm at Peter's Departure. Standing there, watching everyone fall to the ground, watching them all die.

I see the cliff and the clouds, I see you and I see the Vessel. It frightens me. Do you think these dreams are important?"

Lillian paused for a moment, eyebrows furrowed. "I do not know Mya; but I do know that you should trust your dreams. Mya, I'm getting tired, would you mind?"

"Of course not mother. I will be back in the morning. Get some rest," said Mya, kissing her mother's head. Lillian smiled.

"Thank you Mya."

Standing and walking toward the door Mya turned back to her mother.

"We will find him right?"

"Of course dear . . . I know it in my heart," said Lillian, glancing over the puffy bedsheets toward her daughter. Mya smiled, a short and tight smile, then left the room.

Alone, Lillian's smile faded. She turned her head and gazed out at the sea. On the far distant horizon she noticed the faintest touch of grey, clouds and storms roaming across the sea. She closed her eyes.

"Have I made the right choice," she whispered, her voice quivering under the storm tormenting her tired mind . . . her mind . . . delicate eyes closing . . . drifting into memory.

Departure One

Mya

"Of course I remember it. It was only a few years ago. I suppose a lot has happened since the funeral, but that makes no difference. I have never seen my mother so distraught; in fact, she didn't even shed that many tears at my own father's funeral. But to lose two husbands like that . . . it's no wonder her health has only gone from bad to worse these past few years."

And I do remember it. I remember it very well. I feel like I have become a new person since then. It's been nearly two years since Peter Smith died; a man I hardly knew, a man from Earth. But he was Michael's father. I'm still not sure if Michael even knows about Peter's death. No one has seen him in so long . . . but regardless, the funeral I certainly remember.

It was shortly after the tragic and historic series of events at the Cerulean School. I remember his eyes . . . burning in the inky darkness of that Chamber, the Culling Chamber it had been called. I remember them coming towards us, glimmering with anger and something else, something like glee. Everyone I loved was in that room; Michael, my mother, Quixitix, Dunny . . . we were all there, strangers to this newly formed creature staggering toward us. We did nothing to stop it. I suppose we had no choice, but there is always choice, right? I can remember my half brother floating, flying, just like he had done when he saved me from Teague in the woods, above that room, Allcraft circling after him, Teague fending off those strange, jagged-toothed creatures, and Bartlebug trying to kill my mother again. It's funny really. It's so blurry now, that room and those people, it all feels like one long dream, one strange and terrible nightmare. But the world is quiet now. We all thought Allcraft would bring chaos and destruction with him from Twilight or wherever he had been taking refuge for all these years but instead he has just disappeared; and Michael with him. Anyway, Peter's funeral.

"Mya, come here." I remember my mother's voice quivering when she called me over, a strained warble that sounded nothing like she used to.

"Hello mother," I said. I tried to keep my voice as formal as possible; as womanly as possible. I knew she needed my strength and I wanted to give it to her but my heart was heavy too.

"Do you remember your father?" she asked me.

"Of course I do, well, the good times anyway, before Bartlebug."

"Hello m'lady. Sorry to interrupt, just wanted to send you condolences from my family." It was Mr. Mayweather, his wife and his son. I didn't see Madeline so I assumed she was busy with something else.

"Many thanks Mr. Mayweather." My mother shook his hand and they embraced for a moment. I watched her pretend to smile and then they walked away, toward the Cliffside.

"I'm sorry Mya. What was I saying? Of course, your father . . ."

Her voice trailed off and I wondered where her mind went. I watched her head move slightly to one side, I noticed her hair slightly swaying under the grey clouds above, loose ends prickling up here and there, streak marks down her cheeks from the crying, and I wondered what she was thinking of at that moment.

"Do you see those men over there Mya? Those are Orators." She pointed and my gaze followed her extended finger toward a small mound on the cliffside. I watched as three men dressed in long satin robes discussed something together near this mound. The wind from the sea below buffeted their robes and one of them kept brushing the flowing gown down over his legs. Another of them carried a small urn in his hands; mother told me it was only a keepsake, a stand in; we call them Vessels. Nothing had been found at Cerulean to fill it. I kept watching until one of them began to walk toward the Mayweather family standing by the cliff.

"I remember hearing about them growing up." That was a true statement. When I was very young my teachers used to tell us all sorts of things. These particular people were in charge of Departures, as we often call them here, and when a soul departs into the ether beyond Serafina they oversee the ceremony. Although I have a very skeptical mind many believe the Orators share some kind of connection with the Seraphim and they are especially attuned to help the soul make the voyage into their loving embrace. I do not know.

"They were at your father's departure, do you remember?"

"Yes," I said. I turned my face away from her and saw Quixitix and Dunny standing off to one side of the cliff. Quite a mismatch standing there in front of the grey backdrop; the one a tall and skinny stick of a man and the other a giant, wider than three of his brother together. I always enjoyed those two though, never a dull moment. I often recall Dunny sneaking me food when I was a girl at the castle. As I stared at them and waited for my mother to continue, they both looked like shells of themselves; shattered and wasting. And the Mayweathers. Look at the boy, well, he is more like a man these days.

"I used to know one of them when he was a boy, the one talking with Mr. Mayweather." The sound of her voice brought my attention back to her.

"Oh really?"

"Yes. Edgar."

And that was the last thing I remember. The name Edgar. I have been trying to remember what happened next at that Departure, but my mind seems to be fighting against me, like the memory has been stolen or lost, like it's not there. I can feel the space where it used to be though; I can feel an emptiness when I think back on that day. The events seem normal but . . . I don't know. The next thing I do remember is waking up in Aside the morning after the Departure. I asked my mother what had happened but she never got around to answering me. That was the day, the day after Peter's funeral, that the first signs began to manifest.

"So I do remember that day. I remember the loss and the pain and the people. I remember . . . two figures on a hilltop. I remember feeling like something was missing. Does this make sense to you at all?"

▼

IN A MIRROR, DARKLY

She opened her eyes slowly, cautiously. Even in the confused time between dreams and waking the pain returned to her, like a little child coming home whining and moaning. Usually the pain would be far away and then come rushing to the foreground. The woman wanted to go back to sleep but now her entire body began to sing, her nerves wincing with each breath, each tiny movement she made. Things had improved, however. She thought back to the first night, the first night after she lost everything. The Cerulean School had been crumbling around them, her world falling apart stone by stone.

"I can't," she cried.

"Please, Headmistress you must, we don't have time!" Krys shouted, her voice reverberating off the walls of the marble hallway. Another tremor and the three women had to clutch the wall to keep them from falling to the ground.

"The . . . pain . . ." Ja'Mirra, her body ravaged and destroyed from the malicious attack inflicted upon her by the man she once adored as a savior, wanted nothing more than to stop moving and sit down . . . just close her eyes and let the darkness swallow her.

"Headmistress no, we must go now! Krys, get her up!" Cyril approached them, stern and beautiful at the same time, green eyes piercing. "Here." She spoke The Word, her voice calm and confident, and in her hand materialized a small bottle in the shape of a pear. Loosening the cap and retrieving a small dollop of the cream inside, Cyril proceeded to apply the concoction to Ja'Mirra's raw skin. "It will spread by itself; I need only put it in certain places. How does that feel Ja'Mirra?" Ja'Mirra felt the relief instantly.

"Better," she replied. She could feel the cool cream soothing her torn skin and she felt a small surge of energy enter her body. As she began to stand, the Cerulean School again shook around them.

"Please, we must . . . look out!" Krys yelled and flung herself forward; slamming into Cyril and Ja'Mirra just as a massive chunk of marble came crashing to the floor where seconds before the women huddled together.

"Let's go!" Krys grabbed them both and led them down the hallway. They turned a few more corners and soon arrived at the entrance to the school, the massive gold and black doors stood open, small pieces of them crumbling off and falling to the floor. Ja'Mirra happened to notice the intricate designs emblazoned on the door and the realization struck her that this was the last time she would ever see her beloved school . . . she thought that was perhaps the price she would have to pay for her greed and ambition.

"Now!" shouted Cyril. The trio ran toward the door as the school let loose with one massive quake. The black and gold door broke free from its hinge and came slamming to the ground just as the women ran past the entrance. The sound was deafening. Stone and mortar fell all around them as they ran through the courtyard and down the path toward the lake. Finally they stopped and turned around, safely positioned away from the school. Ja'Mirra watched as spires fell like dying soldiers, once mighty pillars of the sky, now toppling to the ground. She saw the ground open and swallow sections of the school; whole buildings where gifted young women used to play and learn, where they would grow and discover who they were. As the tears began to slide down her face she felt them sting the exposed and bleeding skin, the places were Lucas had torn her . . . the pain was worth the price.

"Come, Headmistress," said Krys. Taking Ja'Mirra's arm, Krys led her to the silver lake, now filled with a few floating pieces of debris, and sections of the once magnificent bridge bobbing up and down like buoys.

"Boat," said Cyril, her mind filled with the image of a three person boat, small yet sturdy, made of wood with two oars and three seats . . . the image suddenly became real.

"Let me help you Ja'Mirra," said Krys. The women entered the boat as Cyril and Krys began rowing across the lake. Ja'Mirra took one long and painful look back to her school, watching the remaining structures sink into the soil. She would never see it again. She closed her eyes and everything went dark. She would not open them again for several months.

"I don't even recognize her," said Ja'Mirra, staring into a large, square piece of Twin Glass. "Who are you?"

"Here Headmistress," said Cyril, handing Ja'Mirra a black satin cloth. Ja'Mirra pressed the delicate fabric to her eyes and wiped away the tears. Even those stung. She handed the cloth back to her former student with timid and shaking fingers.

"All I did for him . . . and everything about him was true in the end."

Cyril looked at Krys, a stare indicating how tired they both were of hearing this story over and over again.

"We know Headmistress; he lied to you, he used you, but he could not defeat you."

"Yes, yes . . . I just . . . this isn't how it was supposed to be."

Krys took a deep breath.

"How long has it been Ja'Mirra?" said Krys, her long black hair swaying above her shoulders as she spoke.

"How long . . ."

"Since this happened? Almost two years."

"Krys, stop," interjected Cyril.

"No Cyril, I have to say this. Ja'Mirra, look how far you've come since that day. You were barely alive. Now you are almost ready to get back on your feet and still you moan about Lucas Allcraft."

"But Krys, I . . ." said Ja'Mirra, her voice quivering.

"Still, you complain about how he used you and mistreated you . . . when are you going to accept what he did and move on? Are you going to let him continue to torment you like this forever?"

"Krys, please! I don't think this is the time . . ."

"Cyril! Let me speak! You are the Headmistress of the Cerulean School and one of the greatest Fabricantresses that ever lived! And look at you, starring, teary-eyed into Twin Glass all day and feeling sorry for yourself about Lucas Allcraft. You need to let go of him Ja'Mirra."

As she pronounced the Headmistress' name the fire from one of the torches on the wall sprung to life, punctuating Krys' anger.

"Headmistress, I'm sorry . . ." said Cyril, trying to quell the rage coming from Krys. Krys shot her a devilish look.

"No Cyril . . . you don't have to apologize. Perhaps Krys is right."

Krys said nothing, just stood glaring at Ja'Mirra and Cyril.

Reaching toward her head, Ja'Mirra felt for the end of the bandage covering most of her face.

"Headmistress, what are you doing?"

"It's okay Cyril," said Ja'Mirra, wincing as she began to unwrap the bandage from around her bruised face.

"It's been . . . nearly two . . . years," with each layer Ja'Mirra pulled away she winced from the pain, punctuating her words. "Two years . . . I have been here . . . hurting . . ."

Ja'Mirra dropped a segment of the oily bandage onto the floor near Cyril's feet and continued unwrapping. Krys watched with astonishment as the former Headmistress slowly peeled away the bandage hiding her disfigured face and some of the anger she felt ebbed away.

"Two years I have sat here with him, thinking about him, wishing things had happened differently." Ja'Mirra continued to unwrap the bandage as Cyril watched, helpless.

"But no longer. Krys is right. I have to . . . move on and . . . stop whatever madness . . . that monster is planning."

The last, soft piece of bandage fell to the floor.

"Headmistress I . . ."

"It's fine Cyril."

"Yes," said Cyril as she made her way to the room's exit, glancing quickly over her shoulder at Ja'Mirra who still stared intently into the Twin Glass. As Cyril turned to leave the room, her thoughts lingered on the woman she served for so long, the Fabricantress she had dedicated herself to. Perhaps she had been too naïve to think she could stay with Ja'Mirra forever. Perhaps she had served enough. Cyril opened the door slowly, the sound jarring her from her own thoughts, and left the room, leaving Krys and Ja'Mirra alone in the chamber.

"Krys . . ."

"Yes, Headmistress?"

"I need a favor from you and it is very important."

Krys noticed the hesitation and concern in Ja'Mirra's voice and she waited to hear what she wanted.

"Have you ever been to Blanchfield?"

"Once, when I was a little girl."

"And have you ever seen the castle there, the capital, Blanchfield Castle?"

"Never in person but I have heard of it," said Krys, now turning around to face Ja'Mirra. The Headmistress still stared into the Twin Glass, her face lacerated and dry, her eyes reaching far beyond her own refection.

"I need you to go there for me and . . . retrieve something."

"Retrieve? But what about the Unrest? You know as well as anyone that a person cannot simply walk into a capital city these days . . . the five Overpowers are still reeling from the disaster Teague caused."

"Yes, I know . . . the world is a much more frightening place now but I need you to go there. I imagine it is abandoned now. The citizens of Blanchfield have moved away from the castle. When their king was murdered they left; found new homes. You should not have much trouble."

"Alright then. What is it you need from there?"

"A book. It once belonged to a very good friend of mine; long ago." Ja'Mirra looked to the floor, remembering her friend; the long flow of her golden hair, the way her eyes would shine even in the darkest night. "Seems like a lifetime ago."

"Where can I find it? The book?"

"I'm not sure. Lillian was the Queen of Blanchfield for many years so I imagine the book is still there in the castle somewhere. Most copies of it have been destroyed, lost in the ether of history. This one survived; it is quite rare actually."

"What is it called?"

"The cover is maroon with a stark black binding; leather. The book is quite large and on the cover you will see, emblazoned in spidery-gold writing, the title; The Song of The Seraphim."

Krys looked puzzled, the weight of this important new assignment taking the place of her anger. "The Seraphim? Is it a Holy text?"

"No, not like the ones you are thinking about. There really isn't much to be found there . . . it has mostly sentimental value for me," said Ja'Mirra, glancing to the window.

"Well then I will find it for you, if I can. And Headmistress?"

"Yes, Krys?"

"Take care of yourself." With that Krys exited the room and left Ja'Mirra with only the echoing sound of the door shutting. She looked again into the Twin Glass.

"Who are you?" The face was taught and tight; scars and lacerations covered the once pristine skin. Ja'Mirra's previously ruby lips now appeared only as small pink curves of flesh. "I know who you are," she said to the Glass. "You're not the same person you used to be, but I know you, I see you in there," Ja'Mirra's eyes glowed with fire as she spoke and for the first time since her beloved school crumbled before her eyes she saw that fire ignite again; small and flickering, but there nonetheless. "And it is time he knew you too."

CHAPTER 4

▼

SECRET STORIES

"Torch." The wooden stick materialized in Mya's hand instants after she spoke The Word, an image produced and replicated from the one she had in her head. She deftly lit the torch with some flint and the fiery light sprung up around her. It was easy. She barely even needed to use The Word anymore; she needed only to visualize what she wanted in her mind and the Fabricant would rush through her like a wild wind, soaring from imagination to reality. She wanted to hear her own voice though, needed to listen to the sound, to any sound, especially in this forgotten place.

The light from the torch bounced off the stone walls and danced around her; jesters of flickering light and shadow. She had walked these halls so many times but that felt like a lifetime ago. She passed the dining hall, massive, and remembered eating meals here as a child. Her father had, of course, forbidden her to eat with the rest of the court but she had come here anyway. She liked the sounds of the silverware clinking together and folks laughing; people talking and sharing their lives, the events of the day, someone telling a joke or someone yelling. It all appealed to her very much, the contrast between the dining hall and her father's quarters was like night and day; Mya preferred the night.

As she threw the torchlight upon the hall now, her heart sank. How could it have changed so much? The tables shattered, left broken like crushed bones, pots and pans strewn about, melted from fire or worse, piles of debris and rotting food scattered in decaying and odorous piles . . . it made her heartsick. She continued on.

"How could you all leave like this . . ." she said aloud, her voice clamoring off of the walls of the long, stone hallway. "Just because your king perished . . . how could you abandon your homes?" It was all she could do to keep herself from remembering him as her father; she had to keep her mind in check and refer to him only as king, but her father died long before the king of Blanchfield did. Still, was he the only thing holding these people together? Was he the only thread keeping this kingdom, her home, from unraveling?

Mya knew the answers to her own questions as she asked them, her own voice keeping her company. They left because they were afraid. She had been afraid too, especially in the weeks and months following Allcraft's return. Teague; the once apprentice of Lucas Allcraft, a Magican trapped in time, soul-less, had been the ominous harbinger of Lucas Allcraft. His rage had built for nearly one-hundred years and then he had the opportunity to meet Michael Smith in a forest. This one event, this encounter, had trigged something in Teague, set him loose somehow, grounded him back in reality. Mya supposed it was because Teague realized he was not alone, that he realized other Magicans existed again, and so he set out to unleash the rage Lucas Allcraft had built in him. He started with Mya's father.

"I wasn't there with you, in the end," she said aloud. "After I left with Michael . . . and what Bartlebug did to you all those years . . . I regret leaving you now." She found her way into the throne room as she spoke to the empty halls of her castle. The once regal and ornate décor was now only tatters and ghosts; the deep red carpet burned and torn, the majestic tapestries ripped to shreds. Small rodents and bugs skittered here and there and Mya listened to their hissing and clicking in the darkness. She approached her father's throne. Nothing sat there now except a small broach nestled in the corner of the massive chair. Mya bent down and picked up the trinket, her fingers feeling the coldness of the metal. Had her father worn this? She did not recognize the symbol. "I'm sorry I wasn't there," she said aloud.

Regret filled her like an overflowing vase. On her adventures with Michael she had barely even thought of her father, her anger at his betrayal and alliance with Bartlebug blinding her. Perhaps it was easier to hate than to forgive.

"I wish I had taken the harder road Father," she said to the empty throne room. Her thoughts continued to drift back in time until she heard a noise from an adjacent room; the royal living quarters. The sound cut through the clicking of the insects and Mya immediately froze, her attention snapping back to her surroundings.

Was she alone? She stood, breathless, silent and still, listening for the noise again. She heard something, a different noise, but a noise nonetheless. Someone else was in the castle.

Slowly, Mya crept forward, dimming the light of the torch as best she could. Again, a noise, something like an object hitting the floor. The hallway leading to her parents' sleeping quarters was short but very dark; no light emanated from it and Mya did not risk illuminating her torch any more. She listened again and without doubt the noise was coming from the end of the hallway. Mya continued to walk, slowly and quietly.

Finally, she reached the end of the hallway and the door leading to her mother's private chambers. The door was slightly ajar and Mya could see a small sliver of light pouring from the opening. More noises and now Mya was certain the other person was in her mother's old room. Mya tiptoed to the door and peaked in through the small opening. She saw nothing; only a small candle flickering in the corner. She listened; nothing. Mya held her breath and concentrated on the sounds coming from the room.

Suddenly the door swung open and inward, sending Mya crashing to the hard stone floor. She had been resting her shoulder on the door and when it opened she fell, hard, upon the stone. Her torch flew from her hand and landed on the other side of the room, dangerously close to a massive bear-skin rug covering the floor.

"Don't move," said the voice above her. Mya thought she recognized the voice, a distant and vague memory, but could not place it. "Who are you?" demanded the stranger.

"My name is Mya VanVargott; the heiress of this castle," said Mya, her eyes to the floor. "And who are you then?"

"It does not concern you. You say you are the heiress? Your mother was the queen then?"

Mya said nothing.

"I will accept your silence as acquiescence. I am looking for a book but it is not here. I have searched all these rooms. Tell me, where would your mother keep something very dear to her?"

Mya knew the answer before the strange woman finished asking the question. When she was young, Lillian would bring Mya to her room and tell Mya to cover her eyes. Mya always loved that part and for years she thought her mother had special powers because of what happened next. With her eyes closed, Mya would always hear her mother speak a few words, soft and inaudible, and Mya knew what this meant. Sometimes, Mya would open her eyes early, too filled with excitement to keep them shut. She would see the floor of her mother's room dissolve away like water and in its place a long, spiraling set of stairs would appear, descending down into the depths of the castle. Lillian would lead her daughter down the steps to a very small room below. Mya always loved this room because it was so bright and colorful; nothing like what she expected a secret room below the floor to look like. Instead of the cold stone walls of the castle, this room had soft carpets covering the floor and tapestries adorning the walls. A soft sofa nestled against one wall with large, fluffy pillows upon it. Lights not made of fire stood at different points in the room and Mya had always been amazed at the soft glow they gave off. A rocking chair and a small wooden desk sat in one corner and in the other was the book shelf. The book shelf . . . until this moment Mya had not thought about that bookshelf in years. Now, of course, she understood it. But as a child she was simply amazed by the stories, stories no other child of Serafina had ever heard; stories only Lillian VanVargott could tell her daughter.

"I have no idea what you're talking about," said Mya from the floor.

"Oh I doubt that. How can I persuade you to tell me?"

"For starters you could let me stand up," said Mya, beginning to rise from the floor. The woman suddenly struck her on the neck as she lifted herself, hard, sending Mya back to the ground. She could feel her neck begin to swell immediately.

"Well that isn't going to help you very much," said Mya.

"I don't care. I don't need your help anyway."

Mya heard the sound of the object moving through the air before it hit her, hard, just in the back of the head, and then everything went black.

The sensation of the cold stone floor pressing against her cheek woke Mya up. She had no idea how long she had been passed out but judging from the pain and the large, swollen lump on her neck, she figured it had been some time. She got to her feet slowly; making sure her vision was okay. She could see just fine, aside from the splitting headache that was thundering its way across her brain. Mya soon realized the woman who had attacked her was gone and only silence and the distant sound of dripping water remained. The room had undergone one small change however. Mya's heart sank.

The floor was gone near the center of the room, just in the place Mya remembered it. Somehow, the stranger had found her mother's secret room. Or perhaps the woman was still down there? Mya had no idea, and so she proceeded with caution. Slowly, she crept toward the downward-spiraling staircase in the floor and listened. She heard nothing. She peered over the side of the ledge and looked down. She could just make out the smallest flicker of candle light dancing at the base of the stairs. Mya thought the woman must still be down there, looking for whatever it was she had come here to find. As quiet as she could, Mya began her decent into Lillian's secret room, making her feet silent on the cold stone stairs. She inched closer and closer to the flickering light below, one step after another, breath held, waiting for this mystery woman to appear at the base of the stairs, ready for attack. At last Mya reached the bottom of the staircase. The light was stronger now and it felt warmer down here, which was odd. Her mother's room was just beyond the archway standing before Mya. The light emanated from there and Mya approached slowly, ready to spring upon the woman inside and surprise her. The surprise, however, belonged to Mya.

What she had mistaken for candle light was something much worse; dancing flames. Mya entered her mother's secret room. The room no longer held the interloper; instead a large fire roared and burned in the room's center, quickly making its way to the walls. The heat from the flames buffeted Mya's face and body, singeing the delicate hair on her forearms. Several pieces of furniture had already caught fire and the bookshelf in the back of the room was in immediate peril. Mya acted quickly.

She knew she could not Fabricate water; if she doused the bookshelf her goal would be lost. She needed another solution. Before she could focus on stopping the spreading flame she knew the bookshelf must be saved. Without even speaking, a massive wall sprung forth from the floor and shot toward the ceiling of the room, creating a protective barrier between the encroaching flames and the precious books on the shelf. Next, she needed to stop the fire.

She thought, perilous seconds flying past as the fire consumed the room, pressing against the newly constructed wall in front of the book case. The fumes from the burning fire swirled around Mya and she breathed them in, coughing, knowing she had only seconds before the flames would be too much and the room would be totally consumed. Then the image sprung into her mind and she spoke The Word, doing her best to describe the object. Quickly, the object began to take shape. At the top of the room, a massive, bladed fan appeared and began spinning. Mya threw herself to the ground as the fan spun, sending massive amounts of air surging through the room. Small objects took flight and twirled around the small space, and Mya could feel the hot smoke swirling madly. As the fan spun faster and faster, Mya watched in horror as the flames did not die down but instead grew more intense. Unsure of what to do, Mya stared, terrified at the massive sea of flames making its way toward the bookshelf, beginning to spread around her protective wall. As if reacting to her terror, Mya's mind offered up an image to her, something from her childhood. She could see her mother clearly, soft candle light illuminating her eager face. Mya's view traced her mother's arm, arriving at her hand which held a small, metal rod with what looked like a thimble attached to the end. In her memory, Mya saw her mother place the thimble over the candle flame and the flame died.

Mya needed only to think of the image and suddenly a massive glass dome appeared at the top of the room, replacing the wooden fan Mya Fabricated earlier. Mya jumped out of the way as the glass dome slammed down, covering the entire room and encasing the fire. At the same moment, Mya reshaped the protective wall so it simply encased the bookself, the sound of bending metal reverberating off the walls of the room. With the bookshelf secured, Mya simply waited as the flames devoured the only remaining air inside the glass dome. They sputtered furious for several mintues, consuming everything in the space under the dome except the protectred bookshelf, and eventually the flames began to wither and die. Mya watched them sputter and flicker out, one by one; what was once a raging sea of fire now only a few small, burning notes all because of a simple glass dome. Once all the flames were gone, Mya allowed the dome to disappear as well. She breathed deeply, relieved; some of the lingering ash and smoke filling her lungs. Scanning the room, she surveyed how little she had managed to save; the sofa appeared a charred mess, the desk now a crackling pile of burned wood. Mya approached the bookshelf and removed the metal wall. Miraculously, it seemed all of the books had escaped the fire and were still resting upon the shelf exactly as the intruder had left them. She approached the shelf; the carpet on the floor now burned and ruined, ashy under her feet.

She scanned the remaining books and recognized all of them:

> *Alice in Wonderland*
> *Treasure Island*
> *The Lion, the Witch and the Wardrobe.*
> *A Christmas Carol*

Mya continued to examine the books, books that were never meant for Serafina, stories from another world that Mya had heard countless times as a child; stories no one else in her world knew existed. Other Serafina children heard about *Stuart the Rabbit, Roses in the Mist,* and *The Seven Sigils.* She never thought it then, but now her mind wondered if perhaps she was more like an Earth-born than she had ever imagined. She scanned several more titles; many of the books were tattered and worn with age, one was missing its title entirely and all that Mya could make out on the spine was the image of a red rose inside a keyhole. She stood for several mintues scanning the books, her mind calling up images of her mother sitting in the now ruined rocking chair reading, Lillian's melodic voice echoing around the room like a bottled songbird. As she gazed at the bookshelf Mya saw that each shelf stood full . . . she wondered what her assailant could have wanted here. Then her eyes landed on the third self down, a conspicuously empty space.

"There's one missing," she said out loud. "Mother always kept this shelf full. She loved her books; she would not have let this space go without filling it." Mya ran her fingers over the empty space, thinking, feeling the bindings of the books, rough and leathery, looking at names like *The Hobbit* and *Journey to the Center of the Earth*. Then she realized.

The answer was obvious. Whatever her attacker came here for she had found it and taken it. A book. *Where does your mother keep things that are precious to her?* Was it a book the attacker was after? A book from Earth?

"What could be so important?" thought Mya.

Mya lingered in the room for quite some time, running her hands over the old furniture, chairs and tables made from trees that never grew on Serafina. Her head was throbbing from the trauma of the intruder's attack. All of the furniture was destroyed and so Mya Fabricated a new easy chair; a bit one with comfy pillows and welcoming open space. She fell into the chair, exhausted. Her mind raced over the events of the last several minutes; the fire, the intruder and the missing book. Her mother's room, once a haven from the dangers of the world, now a charred and tattered mess. Without intention, Mya's thoughts drifted off and soon her throbbing head and tired body took control, sending her cascading into the ether of a dreamless sleep.

Ja'Mirra sat in the small corner of her room warming her hands by the fire. The house was far from what Ja'Mirra was used to but Krys had been kind enough to offer her home and Ja'Mirra would not refuse her kindness. Since Ja'Mirra had removed her bandages Cyril had not returned;

her disciple's absence Ja'Mirra took as a bad omen. Her thoughts turned to her other disciple, Krys, hoping her errand would produce the item she needed. As if spurned by her thoughts, the door slowly opened, letting in the cold for a moment. Ja'Mirra turned.

"Did you find what I asked for, Krys?" asked Ja'Mirra.

Krys said nothing. She crossed the room, unwrapped the object from a white scarf, and handed it to Ja'Mirra.

"Excellent," said Ja'Mirra, looking down at the book in her hands. Her fingers slowly moved across the soft binding, feeling every fiber of the tome.

"What is it?" asked Krys. Ja'Mirra smiled and softly spoke the Word. As she did, golden and spidery letters appeared on the cover of the book. *The Song of the Seraphim*.

Krys watched the letters appear from the inky blackness of the book's cover. "The Song of the Seraphim? I thought that was only a legend?"

"Clearly, it is not." Ja'Mirra flipped open the book and peered through the pages, pleased. "You have done very well Krys."

"Mya VanVargott was there," reported Krys. "I knocked her out."

"Not to worry. We have what we need."

Ja'Mirra returned to her seat in front of the fire and let the warmth caress her. She clutched the book tightly to her chest and smiled, the light from the fire dancing on her scarred and glistening face.

"The Song of the Seraphim." She spoke the words only as a whisper, the crackling of the fire drowning her out. "At last." Ja'Mirra opened the book and began rifling through the pages, one by one, reading the sacred text, the secrets of the Seraphim, the secrets she knew Allcraft was after, then she paused. As she looked through the tome, she realized massive sections were missing, in their place only stark white pages, as if the words had been removed. Her joy fluttered and grew dim, like the dying fire before her. She placed the book slowly down on the table next to her chair.

"Krys," her voice, like daggers, cut the room. "We need to pay my old friend a visit."

From *The Song of the Seraphim*

Chapter 10, Verse 17

. . . and she would breathe holy fire unto the world, leaving the mountains and the seas ravished, the leaves dead on the trees, the wind stale on the air, and the sun blotted out. The world, thus, would be born anew and she would give it birth; her words building up the mountains, her words rejuvenating the dying trees, her words breathing wind into the valleys, her words calming the seas. She would be not alone in this; her sisters, by her side, all of them singing, all of them proclaiming to the skies and heavens a new world to be born, a new world to behold, a new world from the lips of the Seraphim . . .

▼

FOOTSTEPS IN THE SNOW

I'm still in here you know. Just because he took my Ember, took my life and my soul . . . he took so much from me but I'm still in here, so listen to me, see me, please!

"Lucious? Here, your dinner."

Mya! Please, look at me! I'm here! I just can't answer you but I'm here! You have to help me; help my sister! Please! Please!

"Here," said Mya, lifting the fork to Lucious' lips. The meat was warm and smelled delicious but Lucious just stared at it, stared like he always did; seeming to gaze at nothing. Mya helped him open his mouth and take the food. He chewed it, mechanically, and swallowed; a mere reflex. The children had been this way since the Culling when Allcraft had stolen their Embers, the very essence of their lives, and left them frail husks, lifeless eyes devoid of light.

Mya! Please, please, please . . . I'm here!

"And how about you Lavinia? Would you like some?"

"Yes . . ." the voice was frail and weak, hardly able to make sounds into words. Mya supposed perhaps the strength of her will was a bit greater than her brother's, perhaps this was how she managed to work with Quixitix on some days in his shop, tinkering with the bits of wires and metal. Mya wondered how Teague had managed to become so powerful after all those years with no Ember, no soul . . . perhaps his insanity eventually won out over his spirit. Mya would not allow the same fate to befall these children.

"Here," she said. Lavinia took the plate and the fork and slowly managed to bring the food to her lips and eat it. Physically, they had grown up in the years following the tragedy at the Cerulean School; Mya certainly noticed the changes in Lucious. His hair, longer now, his face more chiseled, his arms and hands . . . she stopped herself. She could not allow herself thoughts like these, not now, but still, she enjoyed coming to see him. She smiled as she put another spoon full of food to Lavinia's lips.

"Good," said the girl.

"I'm glad you like it," replied Mya. "Have all you want."

Lavinia said nothing, eating silently. The sound of the metallic fork clinking on the porcelain plate echoed in the small bedroom. Lucious only stared.

Lavinia! Can you hear me! Please, hear me! I can't talk, I can't eat . . . I'm helpless. Please, save me sister!

"Very good," said Mya. "Do you want to sleep now?"

Lavinia managed a weak nod of her head, her hair falling in a mess about her brow, the one silver streak standing out.

"Okay. Here you go." Mya helped the twins into bed and tucked them both in. It was odd to Mya to treat them like this; they were about the same age as her and she had to take care of them as though they were infants. She didn't mind though and she allowed herself a few indulgent moments to look into Lucious' eyes as she brought the covers to his chin. Lucas Allcraft had taken something from them they were not prepared to give up. Looking at their pale faces, empty and dark, Mya swore she would reclaim what that monster took.

"Goodnight," said Mya. She bent down and lightly kissed Lucious on the forehead.

Mya; you're kiss is so sweet. You are the only thing keeping me sane, allowing me to exist in this limbo. Seeing you each day . . .

"I will see you both tomorrow," said Mya as she dimmed the light and left the room. Slowly, she closed the door behind her and sighed.

"It's just not fair . . ." she said under her breath. "Two years . . . two days is too long to suffer that fate. Michael . . . how can you do nothing . . . . all this time." She spoke in whispers, only to herself, allowing herself to hear her own words.

"Mya?" the voice clamored down the hallway and reached her ears.

"Shhh," said Mya, placing her finger over her lips in the common gesture of silence. "They just went to bed."

"My apologies." The man's hair was wilder than ever, sticking out at odd angles, some pieces, Mya noticed, were actually longer than others.

"I have some very important news for you," said Quixitix.

"Alright, what is it?"

"Come with me." The professor led Mya away from Lucious and Lavinia's room and down the hallway toward his work area. About a year ago, when Mya began to realize what exactly her brother and Allcraft where up to, she helped Quixitix set up a monitoring station; a place to track Allcraft and find a way to stop whatever plan the Magican set in motion. Their hope had been to stay ahead of Allcraft and Michael; instead they always seemed to be one step behind.

"Have you found another Waver?"

"I think so; and this is a big one."

"Really? Still active?" asked Mya. Quixitix nodded.

"Good. Where?"

"I'll show you," said Quixitix as he opened the door to the lab. The room was very large. Various terminals and work stations were setup at odd places throughout the room. Different colored wires and electrodes ran from one contraption to the next. Most of the items in this room had come from Earth. Mya clearly remembered the look on Archibald's face when she told him about some of the things she had seen there; she was surprised how quickly he had acclimated himself to the technology of Earth. A printer on one side of the room jittered noisily, constantly producing a stream of numbers, and the electrical buzzing of the machines served as a background track to the scene before Mya.

In the center of the room was a large table with various instruments spread out all over it; sextants and rulers, string and protractors; Mya even saw a half-eaten sandwich in one corner. In the middle of the table rested a massive map with haphazard marks and drawings all over it.

"As you know," began Quixitix, "we first became aware of the Wavers shortly after your brother left with Allcraft."

Mya nodded.

"We have since been tracking them, trying to predict where they will happen next, where the fabric between Earth and Serafina will . . . well, waver; become thin."

"Yes, I know all of this professor."

"Yes, but what you don't know is that the Wavers are getting bigger and less stable. It is as if . . . I don't know, as if the wall between our worlds is decaying, and rapidly."

"What's causing it? Does it have anything to do with what my brother is doing?"

"I think so, Mya. Whatever Allcraft and Michael are doing at those Sanctuaries, it is not good. Look at this," said

Quixitix. He walked over to a cloth covered table and removed the sheet to reveal several of the items Mya had brought back with her from the various Sanctuaries she had visited.

"Look at this helmet . . . eh, thing," he said, holding up some kind of facemask brought back from her last expedition. "Do you see the scorch marks here? And the darkened area here?"

"Yes," replied Mya. "What does it mean?"

"It means this was part of something bigger, something that wasn't there when you arrived. Whatever Allcraft did, this is all that was left."

"Is it a mask? Was someone wearing it?"

"It looks awfully painful to be a mask; and look here," said Quixitix, pointing to the jaw area of the facemask. "The lower jaw section is missing but there is a hinge here, as if whoever or whatever was wearing this had a massive, highly flexible jaw. And these sharp protrusions, like teeth, but they point inward, not outward. This thing would be very painful to wear."

"Indeed. What about this new Waver? Have they found it yet?"

"I don't think so," said Quixitix, returning the mask to the table. "But they can't be far off. It just appeared and it is very, very large. The largest so far, I think."

"Where is it?" asked Mya, peering at the map on the large table.

Quixitix hesitated.

"Where is it professor?" asked Mya.

"North. Far North. Anisia."

Mya's face darkened. "Anisia? Are you sure?"

"Yes, I'm sure. You know the stories right?

Mya laughed to herself. "From when I was a girl. I find it hard to believe no one has ever returned though."

"It's true Mya. They call it the Wild North; never inhabited, never settled. The Waver is there."

"Then I'm going."

"Forget it; it's too dangerous. No one even knows what 's up there."

"I don't care. If I can get there before my brother, then maybe I can save him."

"I hope you can Mya but it's too dangerous to go alone."

"I have to go alone; this is my responsibility."

"No," said Quixitix. Mya had never seen the professor so stern, his eyes buried under his bushy eyebrows. "You are not alone. I'm going with you."

"You can't; we need you here to monitor the Wavers and . . ."

"Stop it Mya! What happens if you get hurt up there, or worse? You are going to need friends to help you; you can't do this alone."

Mya looked down and waited a moment, thinking. Perhaps he was right.

"Fine." She hesitated, smiled, "thank you."

"Of course, my lady. When do we leave?"

"Immediately. We have to find my brother and stop whatever he is doing."

Quixitix nodded and looked down at the map. Anisia. He already felt the cold climbing down his spine and he shuddered; not from the chill but from terror.

The Mayweather Family

"Did you ever meet him?" Mrs. Mayweather stood in the doorway, the soft breeze coming in through the open door swirled her red and white dress.

"No, but I have a feeling who he is." Mr. Mayweather sat upon the steps leading to the second floor of their home, buckling the straps on his shoes. The sun, rising from the East and casting a half-wink upon the sleepy town of Aside, told him the day was beginning and it was time for work. Mr. Mayweather knew it would be a long day in the fields but he didn't mind tending to them; in fact, he enjoyed it. There was something fulfilling about working with the land, growing the things that would later find their way into some delicious meal his children would eat. Knowing he had a part in that process made him happy and that is all he ever wanted in this life; a small taste of happiness.

"Aye, I think you're right. People would not understand if she told them who he really was."

"And why should they? A man from another world? Father of her son, a father who was not the King of Blanchfield? People would not understand."

"Do you understand?" asked Mrs. Mayweather, turning and closing the door softly.

Mr. Mayweather looked up from his shoes and saw his wife standing there, the woman who stole his heart as a boy, the woman he loved like no other, and observed her now as the sunlight bounced and played in her long, flowing brown hair. He could see her struggling to understand, doing the best she could; it spread across her face like a hillside fire.

"I don't know. It was love and Michael came from it, so I suppose it can't be all wrong. Besides, she was exiled remember? She would have been killed had she stayed; I remember you and I talking about that right over there all those years ago," he said, nodding his head toward the dining room table.

"Aye, I suppose you're right. Any loss of life is tragic nonetheless. Are we going?"

"I would want to. I haven't seen those folks . . . what has it been, nearly a year now?"

"About that; around the time Madeline left, after we saved Aside from the Bargouls."

Mr. Mayweather looked down and thought of his daughter, hoping her little taste of happiness was near her.

"Where is the service to be held?"

"Not far actually, says here the Lorean Cliffs. That's about half a day's ride."

"Oh, well that settles the matter then, we will certainly go. Is Trevor invited?"

"Yes, it says the family."

"Good," said Mr. Mayweather standing up, "then we shall all go."

He walked to where his wife was standing, her head down. He put his hands on her shoulders, tilted his own head, and looked into her eyes. She looked up at him and they smiled at each other.

"It's sad."

"Aye, death always is," he replied. "But it's the same as the sun or those crops in the field. Life is all made up of comings and goings, arrivals and departures. It's a fundamental idea of life. We are the ones who have trouble accepting that, not the dead."

"You're so philosophical," said Mrs. Mayweather, with a small smile.

"But I'm just a simple farmer," he replied, and kissed her gently on the lips.

———⌇———

They went as a family, together as one unit, all dressed in dire shades of black and grey. They were not unlike the rest of the funeral goers that day; morose and somber people grieving a lost friend. Although many did not even know Peter Smith, a distinct feeling still hung in the air around the Departure site, as though someone dear to the world itself had slipped away.

"Hello m'lady," said Mr. Mayweather. Mrs. Mayweather watched her husband's exchange with the former Queen of Blanchfield . . . that seemed like a lifetime ago. So much had changed since then and so much had stayed the same. Mrs. Mayweather glanced over at Trevor, a man now, a farmer like his father. His innocent smile was still the same at least. The thought gave her hope, hope that innocence and love could still exist in a world with such troubled times.

Mr. Mayweather finished with Lillian and took his wife's arm, leading his family away from the Queen and toward the hillside.

"So tragic. The look in her eyes . . . she seems so empty," said Mr. Mayweather.

"I saw it too. That's what sadness will do to a person."

As the family stood by the cliff, the husband's arm around his wife's shoulders starring out at the sea, one of the Orators approached them.

"Greetings," he said with a somber voice.

"Good day," replied Mr. Mayweather.

"My name is Edgar. How did you know the Departed?"

"He was . . . a friend of a friend I suppose you could say. Good man."

"Indeed, it would seem many good people depart much too soon."

Mr. Mayweather nodded his head.

"If you don't mind, I was hoping you could share a story about the Departed with me. I am putting together some words and I find the best Orations come from those closest to him. Would you mind? Were you close to the Departed?"

"I don't mind at all," said Mr. Mayweather. "Does anyone want to share anything?"

Trevor looked around, wondering if he should tell the Orator what he knew about Peter Smith.

"I have something to say," said Trevor. The Orator looked at him, his red robe fluttering slightly in the breeze cresting the hillside. As he was about to speak Trevor noticed a shape in the corner of his eye, a dark figure on the hillside to their left. The silhouette looked familiar and he had only a moment to register the newly arrived form as the Orator spoke.

"Please, I would be more than happy to . . ."

The world went black.

"Good morning dear," said Mrs. Mayweather.

"Morning mom," said Trevor, sitting down at the breakfast table.

"Are you alright? I know Departures can be upsetting. The ceremony was nice though, the Orator said very nice things."

"I'm fine mom. Busy day, I only have time for something quick."

"Alright," said Mrs. Mayweather, kissing her son's head.

"Any news from your sister?"

Trevor shook his head, biting into a freshly baked piece of cinnamon toast.

"I'm sure we will hear from her soon."

"Me too mom. Me too."

From *The Song of the Seraphim*

Chapter 12, Verse 28

. . . you shall be not alone in this. For all life is connected and all life flows in a circle, forming around again upon itself. Creation and death . . . we are created and then we die. We go back to the ether of the life and from that ether new life arises. Everything is connected in this way; the trees under the burning sun, the stars in the lofty sky the people who touch upon our lives. Remember this, above all else: life is not a singular miracle. It is myriad and it must be connected to other life to prosper.

CHAPTER 6

▼

THE COLD, GREY NORTH

The wagon sputtered and bumped over the rocky hardpan, a path that barely deserved the title of road. The deep greens of the forests on either side would soon give way to sprawling, endless plains of wild beasts, slicing canyons and dark forests; then Anisia, the barren, hostile cold of the Far North.

"She will be fine Mya, Rosemary is an excellent nurse and a good friend," said Quixitix under his bushy eyebrows. He thought about the day he heard about Lillian's illness. The choice had been clear; the woman who had taken care of so many in the small hamlet of Aside, Rosemary, would surely do all she could for the sick Queen. He remembered Rosemary's eyes, green and piercing, aged and filled with wisdom, the day she left Aside and went to be with Lillian. A pronounced bump sent the wagon occupants into the air and roused Quixitix from his thoughts.

The bump caued Mya to let out a small sound of surprise and she glanced at Quixitix from across the wagon. He looked old. She recalled first meeting the eccentric scientist years ago and she recalled seeing a very discernible spark of excitement in his eyes. He had been full of vigor and life then, prepared to help them defend the small coastal town of Aside from the impending Bargoul army and the eventual battle in Couplet Canyon but the professor had changed since those days. He was dimmer somehow, his eyes dark and that spark Mya so vividly remembered diminished. It was still there, but it seemed to be hiding, waiting just below the surface, unable to break through. The events of the past few years had clearly taken their toll on Quixitix.

"Was it that obvious I was thinking about her?"

Quixitix smiled, "I just know you very well my dear. But trust me, Rosemary will look after her."

"Yes, I'm sure she is amazing. Thank you."

"And 'ere we are," said Dunny, making his presence in the small wagon known as he lumbered into the back section of the wagon, having to nearly crawl to avoid the cloth canopy above. "Drink anyone?"

"Help yourself, Dunny," Quixitix answered.

Dunny sat down on the floor-his head just grazing the roof-and unwrapped a large piece of cheese cloth.

"'and me that bottle there, would ya?"

"This one?" asked Quixitix

"Yea, that'll do."

Dunny smiled as his brother handed him the bottle, his eyes wide with anticipation.

"One of my favorite vintages," he said. "Has a bit 'o sweet flavor."

Mya watched him uncap the cork and take a long, lasting swig from the bottle. Dunny motioned toward Mya and Quixitix with the bottle, his eyes almost bright, but they both declined the drink. Mya had far too much on her mind to have it clouded with spirits.

"You feel that?" asked Mya. Quixitix shrugged and looked around. "The breeze. The air. I can feel it cooling down. Do you remember the stories? From when you were a child?"

"Of course, my mother would tell stories of Anisia all the time. I never really believed half of them. Dark magic, enormous beasts, vast, wild ice plains . . . those stories used to make me shiver."

"Me too, when I was a little girl. My father . . . he used to tell me of Anisia in those days when he would say goodnight to me and send me to sleep with a story and a kiss. One in particular keeps slithering through my head." Mya braced herself as the carriage hit an especially large bump. Dunny had been drinking at that moment and some of it got stuck in his throat. He cleared it loudly and continued to sip from the bottle.

"He would tell me stories of a place called the White Loam. Always he would begin with once upon an age . . . and he would speak of the beginning of the world. At first there was only darkness. Vast, empty darkness reaching for all eternity. From within this darkness, against all possibility, emerged the smallest light. A tiny flicker but in such darkness it burned as bright as could be. And it grew. The light grew and grew until finally it outshone the darkness. From this light came the first beings. They were made of it, my father would tell me, made of the light. And these beings created a place where they would be happy. Where they could be away from the vast darkness and live in peace. So they created Serafina and they lived in the White Loam; a place made of light where no darkness could ever reach."

Mya paused and looked up for the first time since beginning her story. Quixitix stared at her intently, his eyes burning brightly under his thick eyebrows. Dunny was also listening but he seemed to be enjoying the contents of the bottle. Mya glanced to the back of the wagon and scanned the remaining two occupants; Lucious and Lavinia. Their eyes were blank, their expressions meaningless.

"Continue," said Quixitix.

"Alright. In the White Loam the beings lived in peace for a very long time. But light cannot exist without darkness and darkness cannot be without light. Eventually, darkness crept back into the world they had created. Some of them even gave into the darkness. They resented the light and wanted nothing to do with their former friends. So they set off on their own, left the White Loam and found another place to live. But the balance was still not right. Both the beings of light and the beings of darkness felt this, my father would say, they both knew that they could not exist forever in this state. Eventually they formed a plan. Both sides knew they needed each other to survive and they soon realized that the only way to remain on Serafina was to strike a balance of light and dark. And this they did but only through a great sacrifice; they had to sacrifice themselves in order to give these new creatures life."

The carriage bounced again.

"Thus the first inhabitants of Serafina were brought into existence. A mixture of light and dark, a being made up of equal parts. Some of these first beings stayed in the White Loam and some ventured out. Those that remained swore to guard the White Loam, to guard the light that still shines there, a beacon and a reminder of the sacrifice of the original people of light and darkness. My father used to tell me these first humans became the Seraphim and still watch over us today, that they were the first to discover how to use the Twinning and they became the Seraphim. He used to tell me that The White Loam is still there, guarded by our great ancestors. Do you think this is true Professor?"

"I think that is a fascinating story Mya and one I have also heard, although my version is not exactly the same, I believe many parts of it. Does the White Loam really exist?

I am not certain. Are there creatures of darkness in Anisia? Of that, I have no doubt. Let us hope that there are also some creatures of light." The carriage rocked hard as if punctuating Quixtix' statement.

Mya nodded and closed her eyes. She wondered which creature she had become . . . one of light or one of darkness? And what about Michael?

"By the Seraphim this is good!" exclaimed Dunny, taking another long swig of the brew.

"By the Seraphim . . ." repeated Mya. "May they watch over us now." Mya reached behind her and opened a small box on a shelf above her seat in the carriage. From the box she pulled out a long scarf, blue and white. Her mother had given Mya the scarf as a present one winter. The fabric was unlike anything Mya had ever seen or felt before. She wrapped it around her neck as the wind began to pick up outside the carriage carrying with it the icy greeting of Anisia.

CHAPTER 7

▼

AN EMPTY STALL

The hallways felt much narrower now; most likely because he felt much bigger. Before, they seemed to encroach upon him, wanting to swallow him up like a tiny fish flapping with all its might against a formidable foe. Now, however, he marched down the dark hallway with intent and determination, without fear of torment or ridicule. He could not remember ever really being in the school after dark before; like most kids he would always go home in the afternoon and his lack of interest in extracurricular activities allowed him to never see this place after the sun set, but now he wanted it all to himself. He had spent so many days here; listening to teachers, doing school work, hiding from bullies. Glancing around at the dented lockers and half-pinned posters, he now realized he did not miss the place very much. Perhaps only the mundane routine of the day, something he certainly did not have now, was the only thing he longed for. He turned a corner and arrived at his destination.

"And here we are," said Michael to the empty hallway, his voice reverberating off the shadowy walls. Michael Smith stood starring at a familiar door, the little white figure in the center of the black circle staring back at him. His mind blossomed with images and memories of the place; troubling to have such vivid memories of a bathroom. He thought about the first time he visited the boy's room, running away

60

from a group of older kids, trying to find a place where they would leave him alone. The last stall seemed perfect. He took refuge there and although the bullies would follow him on occasion, often the smell of the bathroom would scare them away. Michael did not like the smell either but it was better than a bloody nose.

Slowly, Michael opened the door. He first noticed the sound of slowly dripping water. Someone had left the sink on just a little and drop by drop water was escaping the faucet. He focused on the sound, the steady plinking of the water, the way it hit the basin with a tiny, near silent splash. The room was dimly lit and only the faint moonlight coming in through the high, small window allowed Michael to see anything at all. Trash and paper lay scattered around the floor. Three stalls, attached to the wall, stood guarding the place on his right. Three more stalls, each containing a seat, rested just beyond.

"So much has changed," he said again to himself. He glanced in the mirror, twin-glass as they called it at home; at least, the place he now thought of as home.

"I have changed," he said. It was true. His face, older now, bristled, some hairs growing here and there; he looked much older. When he was a boy his hair had been short, now it was long and black, falling upon his shoulders in inky waves. He noticed his own eyes in the moonlight, full of something new as well. Malice? Hatred? Perhaps. Or perhaps they were simply full of emptiness and disillusionment. All the lies; the lies his mother told him, the lies about the Twinning and about Serafina . . . the lies about Earth. Lucas had given him the truth, at last.

"And that is why I follow you. What we are doing is good . . . what we are doing is right." He looked around at the bathroom, the pea-green stall doors, the tiled floor . . . "a joke . . ." he said.

Michael Smith closed his eyes and thought about his first experience moving between the worlds, the first time he shifted, right here in this bathroom. Of course his mind instantly went to Mya . . . the first time he saw her, in that Fabricated rose field, sitting there playing with the delicate flowers. He missed her greatly. The thought of her, of not seeing her for so long, nearly made him decide to not follow Allcraft as the Cerulean School fell around them, but she would have wanted this. She, more than anyone, would have wanted Michael to find the truth, to see what was really behind Serafina, to understand the true nature of the Twinning.

Moving through the dark bathroom, Michael gently felt the coolness of the tile and the dampness of the air. One sink, all the way at the end of the row, appeared ravaged and cracked, one half of the object broken on the floor and the other still attached to the wall. No water poured from this basin. At last he stood in front of his stall, the stall he often visited, his hiding place. He closed his eyes and concentrated. It was so easy for him now, like breathing. He could remember sweating, he could remember thinking about his mother, he could recall thinking he was about to die. As quickly as they came he pushed the thoughts of his mother out of his head. He had no desire to think of her.

Swiftly this time, without much effort and with little push or pull, Michael was back in Serafina. The rose field Mya had once played in was now only dirty hardpan. Michael could smell the desert all around him, acrid and dry, looming like a silent shadow.

"What took you so long?" shouted a voice from afar, the sound amplified by the emptiness. Michael scanned his surroundings and for a moment did not see anyone but he knew the voice and he knew to whom it belonged.

"Just reminiscing I suppose," replied Michael loudly.

"Do we really have time for that Smith?"

Now Michael could see the owner of the voice bouncing toward him, hovering just above the crabgrass and bedrock.

"I really don't think you are in any position to be telling me what to do. After all this time you still think you can talk to me like that Bartlebug?"

Now the Bargoul was close and Michael could see his expression; incredulous yet uncaring.

"I care not. Master Allcraft simply grows impatient and I am sure . . ."

"Tell Allcraft he can wait. I needed to do this."

"Fine, fine. Are you finished then?"

"Yes, I'm finished. It's hard to believe you know."

"What's that Smith?" The Bargoul landed in front of Michael, his bee-body plump and glistening in the moonlight, his pin-prick white eyes large and menacing upon his sooty face.

"What we're doing. Finding the Seraphim and silencing them."

"We are doing what we have to. We are doing what's right. Do you remember what Master Allcraft told you about the Fabricantresses? Have you forgotten their war, their terrible acts to prevent the Magicant from reappearing? To prevent the Magicans from being born? It was all about control, about power. And they thought the Magicans were the ones who could not control themselves."

"I know all of this but still . . . all this time, all the Chambers we have seen, all the voices we've silenced. How is it going to end Bartlebug?"

"I think we both know the answer to that. Now come, Master Allcraft is waiting."

Michael stood motionless, his eyes searching through the desert, looking at the tall mountains rising in the distance, feeling the darkness of the star-empty sky above him, that feeling of hyper-reality he often associated with Serafina. His mind asked him questions about faith and family, about his mother and the terrible sacrifices the Fabricantress Order made in order to stop the Magicant from ever being wielded again. The children, small children . . . their lives ended simply because the world was afraid. Afraid of what? People like Allcraft? People like Michael Smith?

"Smith? Smith, stop staring and let's go."

Michael nodded. He concentrated and spoke the Word, a power he was told could only reside in women of this world; another lie.

"Carriage." The image poured from his mind into reality. A horse drawn carriage appeared out of nowhere, exactly the way Michael had pictured it, something culled from a hodgepodge of cartoons and movies, a cross between Sleepy Hollow and Cinderella.

"I suppose that will do. A Chamber is close, Master Allcraft is already there."

"I know," replied Michael. "I guess it is already nearly gone?"

"Yes, how did you . . ."

"That was how I was first able to come here, from the bathroom at my school. The fabric was too thin, decaying, even then."

"Very well. Come."

The Bargoul buzzed up and into the wagon and Michael decided he would drive the horses under the stars, feel the wind blow through his hair, and think about the end of the world.

CHAPTER 8

▼

ECHOES OF THE PAST

Ja'Mirra listened to the slow, difficult breathing of the woman in the bed. For several minutes the former Headmistress of the now destroyed Cerulean school simply stood watching her old friend, listening to the raspy stiffness of her breath, feeling the last meager rays of sunlight drift through the open window. At last she spoke.

"Lillian, wake up." It was not enough to rouse the sleeping Queen and so Ja'Mirra moved toward the bed. Closer now, she whispered, "Wake up."

Lillian stirred and with dream-like slowness opened her eyes.

"Mya?" she said.

"No, it is not your daughter Lil."

Lillian's eyes widened and began to adjust to the dim light. She soon made out the figure standing over her. If she was shocked or afraid, neither emotion showed on her pale face.

"What are you . . . how did you get here?"

"I came to see you Lillian," said Ja'Mirra, placing her hand on Lillian's forehead.

"But the school, the Cerulean school . . . I thought . . ."

"So did a great many people. But here I am, good as new. You are dying Lillian."

Lillian turned away from Ja'Mirra's touch.

"I know that Ja'. This bed, these people who are kind enough to tend to me each day, all these things remind of that inevitable fate."

"Lillian, I have the book. Krys found it in your room in Blanchfield. But it's not complete. There are words missing Lillian, sections, chapters . . . where are they?"

Lillian managed a small laugh, "I have no idea."

Ja'Mirra breathed heavily.

"Lil, we both know that you have those missing sections somewhere. It is crucial that I find them before Allcraft does."

Lillian did not respond. How could she possibly trust this woman? This friend who had betrayed her, betrayed the Order, and helped to bring the most terrible Magican to ever live back into existence?

"I can't help you Ja'. You need to go. Now."

"You are hardly in a position to order me, my Queen."

"You are right, Ja'. But you're not going to hurt me and we both know that."

"Indeed. I suppose I'm not. Krys?"

Krys appeared from the shadows of the room wearing a deep red gown.

"She won't help us."

"I heard," replied Krys.

"There are other ways. We will find those pages Lillian; with or without your help."

Ja'Mirra motioned with her head for Krys to follow and the former Headmistress swept away from Lillian with indignant resolve.

Krys followed Ja'Mirra from Lillian's bed chamber and like a ballerina, stepped gingerly over the body of the guard she had dispatched on her way in.

Lillian shivered in the cool room, alone now. Had she made the right choice? Even if Ja'Mirra had the book, she could do nothing with it unless she had the rest, nor could Allcraft. Lillian's mind churned, thinking about the plan she had set in motion and praying to the Seraphim she had done enough.

CHAPTER 9

▼

MEMORIES IN THE SNOW

Mya distinctly felt the weather change as the caravan of friends made their way further into the icy folds of the North. She heard the wind kick up and batter the cloth trappings of the covered wagon, listened as the driver moaned from the bite of cold on his skin, tasted the winter frost on her breath. Every noe and then she poked her head from the back of the wagon and watched the landscape change from grassy fields and barren, rolling hills to leafless tress and hard, frozen dirt. She had never been this far North before. Anisia was not far, only a few days journey by wagon, but no one went there due to the harsh conditions and terrible stories. Only the bravest ever ventured to Anisia; hunters usually, glory hounds seeking the fame of bagging some legendary creature. Her father, Charles, had been one of these hunters, before the arrival of Bartlebug. Once, her father had taken her with his hunting party during one of their yearly expeditions. Mya often found herself thinking of her father before Bartlebug arrived on the scene, the way he had been to her, to his people. She remembered the soft feel of his beard on her face, the way he would hug her and pull her close, smile at her with pride.

On this hunting trip, Mya's first, she had felt so proud and special to have been included in something so important.

"Are you warm enough?" He had been so much younger then, as he spoke those words, and Mya only a small girl.

"Yes, father. Thank you." Mya pulled her shawl closer and braced herself against the cold.

"We are not very far now Mya."

He was right. They never went too far North, not nearly as far as Mya's caravan was now.

"Have you ever seen something like this before Mya?" asked Charles, handing his young daughter a piece of tattered parchment. Mya took the offering and examined the drawing etched upon the tan cloth. The beast was massive and fanged, its eyes seemed to glow and pulsate even though Mya knew perfectly well that it was only a drawing. It had fur and a writhing tail which coiled up behind it as if ready to strike right from the etching. Charles could see the slant of fear crawl across Mya's eyes. "Don't worry Mya, you won't come anywhere close to this thing," said Charles, slightly chuckling under his massive hide coat. Mya handed the parchment back to her father and he folded it and tucked it away under his robes.

"What's it called?" asked Mya.

"It is known as an Ostegoth. A foul creation and only ever seen in myth and legend. They say it was created with foul powers, a corruption of the Twinning. No one has even seen one but mayhap we shall bag the beast this day!" said Charles, raising his voice. A few men in the hunting party grunted and hollered in agreement. Perhaps their cheers would not have been so jovial had they know that within the hour their lives would be extinguished.

The sound of Quixitix' voice pulled Mya from her thoughts.

"Are you alright my lady?" asked Quixitix.

"Yes, I'm fine. Just thinking about my father."

Quixitix nodded. "He was a great man, in his prime. A tragic loss. I am so sorry Mya."

Mya nodded. She had barely allowed herself to mourn two years ago, after Allcraft returned, after Teague laid waste to so much. She wondered if she would ever be able to really mourn for her father. Could she mourn him as the man he was or would she have to mourn him as the man he became? She pushed the thoughts aside.

"Certainly is getting cold," warned Dunny from the back of the caravan. The rest of the occupants nodded in agreement.

"We are nearly there, according to my map." Quixitix had been lingering over a large map for most of the journey north, scribbling notes and drawing lines with a straight edge from time to time.

"The source of this latest flux should be close by."

"Do you think we are in time?" asked Mya.

"I do Mya. We will find him this time."

"Professor?" asked Mya. "Do you believe in the White Loam?"

Quixitix laughed. "I am a man of science Mya. There is simply no empirical evidence to suggest such a place exists. I just can't put much faith in something so . . . improbable as the White Loam."

Mya nodded. "I suppose you are right."

A voice from the front of the carriage interrupted the conversation.

"I think you should come look at this . . ."

Mya heard the horses neigh as the reigns were pulled and the carriage slowly stopped. One by one the passengers filed out of the back of the carriage. Bundled in layers of clothing, they were well prepared for the biting cold that waited for them.

"Look there," said Quixitix as they made their way to the front of the carriage.

In the distance rose a massive shape, looming above them, nearly obscured by the blowing wind and light snow. Silhouetted against the grey sky, the structure looked like a massive sword plunging into the ground.

"What's that then?" asked Dunny.

"I do not know," replied Quixitix, "but I think that is what we are looking for. How has something that massive gone unfound for so long? It doesn't make any sense."

Mya thought for a moment, staring at the enormous structure, dark and foreboding in the snow storm.

"Dunny, would you mind bringing Lucious and Lavinia out here to see this?" asked Mya.

"I don't mind, but what for?"

"I want them to see it," replied Mya.

Dunny did as he was asked and moments later the two far-eyed children stood beside Mya, starring into the cold distance.

"Lucious, have you any idea what that is?"

The boy just stared for a moment, his opaque eyes starring far off into nothing, looking at nothing.

"It's no use Mya. Without Embers . . ."

"I know Quixitix. I see them every day and I am reminded what Allcraft did to them. I know what it must be . . ."

"It's there . . ."

The words were almost inaudible in the wind.

"What?" said Mya, kneeling so that she was face to face with Lucious.

"It's there," he repeated.

"What Lucious? What's there?"

The boy pointed to the structure in the distance, the cross-shaped shadow sword.

"Our Embers . . . our souls are there. I can feel them . . ." said Lucious. He then fell silent leaving only the sound of the empty wind swirling around them.

"Thank you Lucious," said Mya, nodding to Dunny. Dunny ushered the children back into the wagon.

"We were right professor. This is it."

Quixitix nodded, "I think you are correct, Mya."

The group crowded back into the large wagon and proceeded onward, toward the mysterious structure as the freezing wind kicked ever stronger.

CHAPTER 10

▼

THE DARK CARESS OF DREAMS

Mya dreamt despite the cold and noisy wind outside the tent. She had Fabricated tents for all of them before the sun fell behind the distant mountains to the West. Mya's tent was sparse and bare, only a small fire burning in the center, the smoke escaping through a tiny hole in the roof, and her cot nestled in one corner. Under the covers the woman turned and tossed, restless and filled with images behind her eyes.

In one she was running and then falling, chased by the Ostegoth from her memory, the beast that had so deftly killed her father's friends that cold day when she was a girl. It was a cycle, repeated, in which she would flee and then fall from the same cliff and plummet toward the same body of water, yet instead of fear she felt like the sky, open and excited, waiting to hit the cold waves below.

In another she was back at the Cerulean School in the Culling Chamber. Again, repeated like a flickering candle flame, she watched as Lucas Allcraft tore the souls from two helpless children, her mind interpreting what it must have been like for them, seeing their own essence, their own Embers, pulled away and taken so casually. In the darkness she heard Allcraft laugh and could see his burning eyes in her mind.

Another dream took her back to where she considered all of this to have started. She stood in her rose field; a childhood place, a place of happiness. The memory of her roses calmed her and she felt at ease. Then the sky darkened and the roses all wilted; they dried out and fell to pieces like burned paper.

"I'm sorry for this Mya," said a voice.

"Look at my roses," she replied.

"Yes, I am sorry for all of it."

"Then why did you do this? Why did you leave?"

"I had to. I had to find my own answers . . . I had to . . ."

"I don't care what you had to do Michael! I have answers, mother has answers, but you chose him. You chose Allcraft." Michael Smith appeared as if out of nowhere, standing next to her in the field. He looked much older, dark and dressed in black from heel to crown.

"Mya, it's not like that."

"Yes it is brother," said Mya, standing and letting a few pieces of a rose fall between her fingers.

"No, Mya. You don't understand. What Allcraft told me . . . the reason I had to go with him . . ."

"I don't care Michael. Don't you understand? No matter what he tells you, no matter what he promises you, he is the villain, the enemy."

"Then what about the Magicans Mya? What about all those children that the Fabricantresses murdered? What if Allcraft is right?"

"Michael! He's not! Look in your heart," shouted Mya, turning to her brother and seeing him for the first time, "look in *my* heart!"

Michael Smith stood in the rose field a shade, a shadow of the boy he once was. His long, dark hair hung around his shoulders like flowing ink and he had dark circles under his eyes.

"Mya, look at this."

Michael spoke the Word and a rose appeared in his hand.

"But how . . ." Mya, speechless, was unsure how to react.

"Much of what you have been told is lies Mya. The Order lied to you. This is why I had to leave you all. I had to find the truth on my own."

"Then come back, now that you have found it."

"I can't."

"Why not!" Mya shouted at her brother, her voice somehow echoing in the empty field.

"I have work to do. A truth so great . . . a truth so dangerous this world is not yet ready for it."

"And what might that be brother? Another lie Allcraft told you?"

"This is no lie Mya. You will come to see soon enough. Be careful in the White Loam. He is waiting for you. He wants you dead."

"And what about you? Do you want me dead?"

Michael looked down for a moment and then his eyes locked with Mya's.

"I love you Mya. I only want to open your eyes . . ."

". . . open your eyes. Open your eyes."

Mya woke as the voices overlapped in her dream.

"Who's there?"

"Me," said a meager voice.

"Lucious?" As Mya's eyes adjusted she saw Lucious standing over her bed, his face illuminated by the dancing light from the small fire. Mya wasn't sure if it was because of the dream or because she was still half asleep but for the first time she noticed how handsome Lucious had become these past few years, his face illuminated by the firelight. Older, darker; he was no longer the boy she knew when they first met.

"You have to open your eyes Mya."

It was the most he had said in ages. In fact, until today, Mya was unsure if Lucious even had the capacity to speak anymore. Perhaps because he was in such close proximity to his Ember . . .

"Lucious, why?"

"You have to see the truth."

Mya thought for a moment that perhaps she was still dreaming, hearing her brother's words echoed back to her from Lucious.

"What truth, Lucious?"

Lucious bent over her cot and kissed her forehead, gently. Mya noticed the softness of the boy's lips on her skin. Then he rose and left the tent, left Mya alone with his cryptic message.

She lay awake for the rest of the night, thinking about Michael and what he had said in the dream as the dream slipped away and Mya could remember only fragments and feelings.

"He is lost. I have to find him. I have to save him."

These were the last words she spoke before sleep overtook her again and she rested for the few remaining hours of darkness, an icy darkness wanting nothing more than to break in, quell the meager fire and leave nothing but endless night in its wake.

From *The Song of the Seraphim*

Chapter 5, Verse 17

. . . and she led them through the world; out of the darkness and into the light. She led them away from the beasts that roamed the land and the creatures inhabiting the seas. They looked to her as savior, with true eyes and true hearts. They saw her as the light in the darkness, shining for them, leading them into the light. This is what has been and this is what yet shall pass.

PART 2

From *The Raleigh Observer, page 16*A

A new viral video has taken the internet by storm this week. Julia Myers, 14, captured the video from her cell phone as she sat in the backseat of her parents' car while traveling in Roanoke, Virginia. "These people just started coming out of the woods along the side of the road and my dad pulled over because they just started walking into traffic," said Myers.

The video, which shows a large mass of people stumbling from a dense forest next to a major highway in Roankoe, could be another example of the popular "flash mobs" that keep popping up in different places around the country. However, no flash mobs have ever gone this far. Deputy Sheriff James Winthrop arrested several of the jay-walkers but many more simply ran, screaming. "I have never seen anything like it. I'm not sure if this was some kind of performance art thing or what, but these people were all dressed up like colonial settlers or something," said Winthrop. "Some even had muskets and old pots and pans. If this was just some kind of hoax, these people at least did their research."

The video can be found all across the web but some online commentors have one very interesting theory about the origin of these mysterious people.

According to user StoryHistory113, "they are the lost colony. Just look at the video! Their garb is pre-colonial, there are children with them and the woods they emerged from are only 10 miles from the site of the infamous Lost Colony of Roanoke. Have they been hiding in those woods all these years, generation after generation?"

Of course, this theory seems a bit far-fetched. When questioned at the police station, one of the mysterious strangers was too shocked to speak, and only kept repeating one word over and over again. "Croatan! Croatan!" This word, of course, was famously carved into a tree near the infamous lost colony. With origins in the language of the Native Americans, this word has no real meaning but was the name of a tribe located along the coast of North Carolina during the 16th century. Although no one really knows what the word means, many scholars believe the literal translation means 'same' or 'mirror image.'

Departure 3

Edgar Bellows

Edgar noticed Lillian talking to her daughter Mya but pretended not to. He was a professional and he made it his point not to take part in the small talk and mingling that inevitably occurred before a Departure ceremony. He did take the time, however, to think about how little Lillian VanVargott had changed since she was a girl. Her name had changed, of course, after she married the King, but Edgar remembered another little girl; one of his best friends. Little Lil Brookhaven.

"Edgar, come on we're going to miss it!" The girl, perhaps only ten or eleven years old, smiled over her shoulder and ran, light-footed, through the grassy field. The spring had just settled over the hills and forests in Blanchfield and Lil was always most fond of this season. Soft nights, warm winds ushered across the rolling hills like cradling hands, and the fire-bugs were in full flight. She saw them beginning their twilight dance as she pranced through the grassy field, watched them make perfect curves of amber light as the sun faded to a crisp and soothing ember on the horizon.

"I'm coming! And we're not going to miss anything," called Edgar, picking up his pace to match with Lil. He watched her smile and run faster toward the large tent in the distance. The tent stretched, curving, toward the orange sky, its flags whipping in the soft breeze. The colors, augmented by the sun's light, were bright and intoxicating. As they drew closer, the duo began to hear faint music, laughter and the sound of clapping. After a few moments Edgar caught up to the girl and they both approached their destination just as the sun began to set beyond the mountains far to the West.

"Amazing . . ." said Lil, gasping for breath.

"It really is Lil," said Edgar.

"Welcome, welcome children. Please, this way! Don't want to be late, do you?"

"No sir," said Lil and Edgar.

"Well then hurry, hurry! The show is about to start!"

Lil and Edgar ran past the large man who had greeted them and passed through a series of cloth doorways, vestibules of a much larger tent, until finally they were under the open sky once more. In the center of the massive structure was a large, open field and, forming a semi-circle from one side of the field to the other, the stands rose up around them. Thousands of people sat there already, waiting patiently for dusk to fall. From the noble people in the city to those who dwelled in the poor outskirts of Blanchfield, the circus was the one event that brought them all together. Lil could see the nobles easy amongst the common people; their dress seemed to be on fire with color and stood out among the drab rags of the poor. Blue orchids and orange sunbursts littered the stands closer to the action, the seats reserved for the nobility. Fancy hats with feathers, glasses too big for faces, collars that stretched all the way to the back of the head; these were only a few of the strange fashion trends Lil noticed as she gazed around the tent, watching the crowd quiver with anticipation and listening to their cacophonous roar. The noise was raucous and free, a din filled with joy and anticipation. In the center of the inner field was a large wooden stage with black, satin drapes hung around it in sleepy cascades. Lil could see a few people moving quietly and quickly upon the stage, but her first order of business was to find a seat for them before the festivities began.

"This way Edgar, follow me."

"Are you sure? I think we would have a better view if we went this . . ."

"Trust me, this way." She took his hand and he felt a rush of something, as he always did, that he was simply too young to fully understand or comprehend but the excitement built in him just the same.

"Do you remember last year Lil?" asked Edgar as they walked together.

"Of course. Remember the fire-breathers? Those were my favorite."

"Yeah, they were really something."

"How about here?" Lil pointed to two empty seats in between a slender woman wearing a dark red cloak and a large man with a huge box of puffed corn. They were close to the circus floor, an area reserved for nobles, but Lil hoped they would go unnoticed. The large man offered them a wide grin and casually offered Lil a handful of the puffed corn. She smiled graciously and took it, handing some to Edgar. Edgar, not used to the combination of salt and sugar, started at the explosion of taste but soon devoured his entire portion. They sat down at last. "This seems good," said Lil, content with her seating choice.

"Seems fine to me."

The children took their seats just as the first celestial stars of the night began to peek their way through the inky veil of the sky and stared, excited and waiting, at the massive stage sitting under the open sky. Suddenly, flames began to burst into life all around the arena, forming a concentric semi-circle of light which encased the stands and illuminated the entire inner-field. A roar of excited cheering erupted from the stands as the spectators watched each flame spout forth.

"Welcome, welcome. Children . . . adults . . . youngsters, hipsters, nipsters and friends!"

The crowd responded to the new voice filling the arean with cheers and shouts. They watched a man make his way into the center of the massive, open space and all eyes were fixed on him.

"What have you come here for on this fine, summer evening?" The man's voice boomed around the arena, filling the space easily.

Some people shouted "give us the Saltgats!" and others answered the man with cries of "Fire-snakes! We want Fire-snakes!" Still others, and seemingly the majority of attendees, yelled with great passion, "we want the Flying-men!"

With a wave of his massive hands the man in the center quieted the crowd. After a few more moments of shouts and cries, the field fell silent. All that could be heard was the sound of the crackling flames in the flambeaus lining the in-field.

"All of this and more you shall have but first, if you feel so kind, feast your eyes on this!"

Lil and Edgar waited patiently for what the man was about to bring forth from the shadows of the large tents standing near the in-field. What they saw shocked and amazed them.

A creature, the most massive creature both young children's eyes had ever had the joy of gazing upon, majestically strode from behind a massive curtain. Lil had heard stories of these growing up, tales of faraway lands filled with exotic beasts and strange creatures. This one, grey and enormous, had a huge snout flowing down from its forehead which, according to Lil's eyes, seems to stand as tall as a Blanchfield Castle parapet off the ground. The creature let out a loud noise, pulling its strange, floppy nose into the air, and the crowd cheered.

"That's called an Elephant," said Lillian to her companion. Edgar nodded.

"I've heard of those. Never thought I'd see one though."

As the children spoke, several performers began to emerge from the back of the inner circle. They wore onyx robes and their faces, half-covered with cloth masks, revealed only their burning eyes. Each one produced a baton of some kind and began throwing and twirling them into the air. Suddenly, the ends of the batons sparked into flame and the crowd roared yet again. When the roar reached its climax, the performers began dancing around the Elephant, spinning in fiery circles and moving with impossible speed and precision. Edgar and Lil were fixated, mouths cracked into everlasting smiles, watching the show spreading out before them. In the distance, unheard by the cacophonous crowd, a thunderclap made its presence known.

"Lil look!" shouted Edgar, pointing at the Elephant.

The performers were now tossing one another high into the air, spiraling through the night sky, over and around the Elephant as the majestic creature pounced through the arena.

"They are amazing," said Lil. Edgar nodded in agreement. The Elephant, covered in massive blankets flowing with red and gold, moved through the circus arena with a massive grace, like a planet unto itself spiraling into infinity. Above, the clouds began to darken and again a sound of storms filled the air.

Now the thunder was closer, and this time the spectators heard the rumbling but ignored it. The show must go on. Lil and Edgar did not pay attention to the thunder either, too enraptured by the fiery dancers and the Elephant to mind the weather. And then it happened.

As if conjured out of nothing, dark clouds covered and blotted out the night time stars and the sky opened, releasing a downpour onto the unsuspecting crowd. The burning pyres did not go out though, as the fire they produced was much too hot for a summer rain shower to thwart. The ground on the infield, however, was not so resilient. As the crowd tried to decide what to do, some fled, some stayed rooted in their seats unaffected by the pouring rain, the performers continued the show. The Elephant paraded around the arena and the fire-twirlers continued throwing their batons and themselves high into the wet air. Some of them even managed to climb onto the back of the Elephant and stood upon the creature twirling, firey streaks blazing through the air.

"Lil, I'm getting soaked!" said Edgar, half excited and half dismayed.

"Me too, but who cares? I say if they are still going then we should . . . ."

Lil could not finish her sentence. As she spoke her eyes happened to glance at the Elephant, now very close to her side of the stands, and the events that unfolded in the next few moments would shape and change not only the world these two children called home but another world, hidden and unseen, far beyond the realm of Twilight.

The rain had made the infield wet and soft and the Elephant, such a massive creature, was slipping. Because of this, the performer riding upon its back could do little to maintain his balance as the creature lunged and swayed.

Lil watched the entire thing play out, knowing what was happening before it actually did and knowing there was nothing she could do.

The performer lost his balance, fell, and dropped his fiery wand. The massive tapestry that had been thrown over the back of the Elephant was the unlucky target of the dropped baton and immediately caught flame, immune to the pouring rain. The creature yelled, bellowed, and began to run. When the crowd realized what was happening their cheers turned to screams, horrified and terrified at the same time.

Now, with a flaming back and a wildly thrashing snout, the Elephant charged forward, heading directly for the stands.

"Edgar, Edgar!" was all Lil could manage as the wild Elephant charged them, aflame, a massive burning terror in the pouring rain.

"Lil, we have to run, we have to!"

Everything seemed to slow down for a moment and Lil saw the people below them in the stands, clustered, and trying desperately to escape the incoming Elephant. There were simply too many of them and they could not move; Lil knew they would surely be killed as soon as the Elephant hit the stands. In those few seconds, something deep inside the young girl flashed to life for the first time, sparked not by her imminent danger but by the peril of others, in that moment her will to save them took over.

Edgar watched everything, and even later as he tried to describe to the women from The Order exactly what Lil had done, he found it difficult to put into words. Her body seemed to glow in the night, glow with a pure white light that seemed brighter than all the stars in the sky. Slowly at first, an angelic beam seeped from the girl's chest and, in a line as straight as the horizon, made its way toward the Elephant. The beam sped up as the Elephant ran closer to the stands, their intersection inevitable. Edgar watched, amazed, and as the beam at last arrived in front of the stands the Elephant was inches from it, charging at full speed. And then it was there, and everyone knew what it was, but none of them believed it really existed.

"By the Seraphim . . ." some said. The crowd, shocked into silenced, observed the scene before them as the quiet rain poured down.

"It's the Shield of the Seraphim . . . ." The sound of the Elephant smashing into the object Mya produced was soft and dull; not the crashing sound that would have erupted had the creature destroyed the wooden stands. When it hit, the Elephant reared back and staggered, then fell to his knees and finally the ground. The performers and workers from the circus rushed to the creature and managed to douse the fire quickly, saving the Elephant but no one seemed as transfixed by the exotic creature as they had been moments before.

The Shield remained for a moment more, a blinding, bright wall of white light, letters and symbols etched into nothing, shining forth from the Shield, and the Elephant, now being doused by the performers, writhed on the ground. Then the light faded and slowly disappeared. The Shield was gone. The onlookers from the crowd followed the path of the beam as it faded and saw it emanating from a young girl. None of them could believe it. This was something only talked about in legends, myth and faith.

"Lil . . . ." Said Edgar, but Lil did not hear him. Her closed eyes saw nothing and her mind was far away. Something else had taken over. The Seraphim had saved those people through the power of the Fabricant.

Seconds later the beam of light was gone and Lil lay crumpled, exhausted, on the stands, the rain falling on her body as her friend Edgar tried to wake her up.

That was the last time Edgar saw Lillian for many years. As word spread of what she did, many women from The Order came to see her. They talked to her friends, her family and soon they decided she was to travel to LochBarren to study with a Fabricantress. Edgar never forgot that night, under the summer sky and the warm, summer rain; the smell of wet grass, the flames, and Lil. That was last time he saw his best friend until the day her husband was to be sent off.

"And so we join together, as one voice, as one heart, to send this loved one to eternal peace." Edgar addressed the crowd, his voice echoing over the roar of the ocean and the sound of the evening wind. The sun had begun its descent and it cast lingering rays of warmth and light upon the faces watching him.

"Peter Smith, beloved companion and friend, may now return to the ether of life, to the source of all goodness, to the warm and welcoming waters of the sea of eternity." As he spoke, Edgar made several motions with his hands, his long cloak mimicking the movements. He saw the pain and sadness on the faces before him, saw the tears on Mya's cheeks and on her mother's, and wished nothing but to grant his friend solace and peace. The crowd was close to the Cliffside, staring at the casket of Peter Smith, adorned with a glorious effigy of the Seraphim, as was customary, and far in the back, standing alone on the last hill before the cliffs, a figure hidden by shadow. Edgar noticed all of this in seconds and continued his Oration.

"Please, friends. Open your hearts to each other today. Open your hearts and allow the memory of this man to rest there, to rest with each of you. Some of you knew him well. Others, only as a name. Others still are here only as a force of peace and solace in this trying time. But all gathered here please remember the name Peter and, in your own way and in your own heart, allow his memory to rest and be at peace."

Edgar, feeling his words were enough, began to move toward the casket and complete the Departure. The last thing he saw was Lillian's face and the figure in the black cloak and then he, along with all the others standing on the cliff, fell to the ground unconscious. The following day, Edgar spoke with his family about the Departure and told the story of how the ceremony went off without a hitch.

Chapter 1

▼

Cyril

As Mya VanVargott and company made their way north to the barren and desolate land known as Anisia, a woman named Cyril made her way to a far more hospitable location.

"Cyril! It has been ages!" said the woman behind the fence as Cyril made her way along the dirt road. When she saw the woman, now older but still with the same bright smile, Cyril could not help but follow suit.

"Margot!" said Cyril, rushing toward the woman. Margot had been tending to a few chickens who perked up at Cyril's approach; several letting out protesting squawks.

"It's been ages since you left for school! Look at you now, a grown woman back to see your home!"

They embraced over the fence, Cyril placing her pack on the floor. The mention of school brought Cyril's mind back two years, back to the night at the Cerulean School when she had decided which direction her life would take. She had barely made it out alive.

"It's great to see you Margot. How is Malcolm?"

Margot shook her head, looking at the ground. "He passed about a year ago dear," she said.

"I'm so sorry," replied Cyril.

"Aye, thanks. It's just been me tending the farm since he's gone. But let's not linger on that. I'm sure your mother will be dying to see you. Are you a full fledged Fabricantress now, then?" said Margot, sizing Cyril up from foot to top.

"Indeed, something like that," replied Cyril, picking up her pack from the ground. A rather large chicken squawked and jumped up, flapping its wings, as Cyril lifted the parcel.

"I 'magine she's down by the market this time of the morning. You should find her there."

They embraced once more and Margot left Cyril with a bright and filling smile as they parted.

Cyril had been just a girl when she was sent to learn the ways of the Fabricant at the Cerulean School and it had been a very long time since she had been back to Bouresque, the town she thought of as home. The city itself was much different than Aside; here things were slower and less full. The people moved at an easy pace and worried not about the cares of the world; here your neighbor looked out for you and life was peaceful. As she walked, Cyril saw many familiar faces and many new ones; young children new to the community and several old folks she had known her whole life. With the sprawling wheat fields to her left, Cyril made her way through the town proper, past the ornate fountain (erected hundreds of years ago but a rather fortuitous stonemason) and finally found herself at the town market.

People moved around and through the market but it wasn't busy despite the amount of people. Everyone said hello to each other, told stories, caught up with the latest news from each of the families and bartered and traded for the goods they needed for their meals that night. Cyril could not help but smile. After the nightmare she had been through at the Cerulean School and the two years since its demise, this was perhaps the only sight that could have brought such as smile to her face. Then she saw her mother.

There she stood, bright blue dress shimmering in the sunlight, red hair falling around her shoulders in untidy bushels. In the crook of her elbow was a small basket filled with vegetables and various other sundries. She looked exactly how Cyril remembered; radiant and beautiful.

"Hi mom," said Cyril above the noise of the crowd. Shayan turned around immediately.

"Cyril?" Her voice trembled, surprised and excited.

"Hey mom," said Cyril, smiling. Shayan rushed toward her daughter and scooped her up in her arms, despite the fact that Cyril was a full grown woman now. A few onlookers smiled and some even clapped.

"You're home, I can't believe it!" said Shayan.

"It's great to be here mom. It's been a long time."

"When I heard the rumors about the school . . . I didn't know what happened to you. I have been worried but I knew in my heart you were okay. Where have you been since the school?"

Cyril thought for a moment and answered. "Around. But I'm here now mom. I'm home for good." Shayan nodded and did not push the issue.

"Come then. Something special for supper tonight. We can make your favorite."

Cyril smiled. "Haphen and rice? I still can't resist."

"Good," replied Shayan. "And I have a gift for you. Something . . . very precious."

Cyril looked at her mother quizzically, wondering what the gift could be.

Arm in arm, Cyril and her mother walked through the market and collected what they would need for the meal that night. For the first time in many years Cyril felt safe and warm, comfortable and at peace.

If only feelings like that could last.

CHAPTER 2

▼

ENCOUNTER IN THE WOODS

"It looks more like a parapet I guess," said Mya. The troop had been walking for the better part of the day and the blistering cold was no friend to any of them. In the distance behind them footprints of various sizes marked their progress, winding across the white blankness for a few miles back and up over a sloping hillside.

"Yes, and it is so massive. How could anyone have built this?" said Quixitix.

"Maybe it was the Fabricant," replied Mya, her face numb even though the scarf she wore covered most of it.

"I suppose you could be right. How is it still standing then? Surely the Fabricantress who created it perished long ago."

"I don't know," said Mya.

"Seems about the right size 'fer me," commented Dunny. The snow seemed to bother him little.

"Do you really think this is the White Loam? Like in the stories?"

"I do Mya. But I do not think this is the source and origin of all life on Serafina. I simply think this was the first place people began to realize they could tap into the Fabricant and the Magicant. Perhaps this is some kind of elemental nexus or a place where the ether of the Twilight flows especially heavily into Serafina. Either way, I do not think we will find any fabled angels or demons in there." The old scientist shivered as if still uncomfortable with the notion of The Twinning and shook the cold from his shoulders. Mya watched him gaze up at the massive tower looking before them and noticed Quixitix looked stern and a little afraid as he stared through the snow at the White Loam.

As they grew nearer, Mya began to see more details and features of the White Loam take shape. It was not shaped like a sword as she had originally thought but instead looked more like a tower from her father's castle. The structure seemed to reach so far into the sky that the clouds obscured the upper most portions of it. Faintly, Mya could make out windows and balconies dotting the outside of the building and from some of these she thought she saw the slow dance of flickering candles.

"Is that where we are going?" said a faint voice. It was Lavinia, her eyes fixed on the tower. She seemed unaffected by the cold but her lips were tinged with blue, like soft powder.

"Yes Lavinia. Hopefully we will be able to help you there. Help you . . . find yourself."

"I hope so too," she said with that same dull, placid voice. Lucious trailed behind his sister, his footprints close together in the snow. He did not speak.

Suddenly, Quixitix motioned for them to stop and placed his hand in front of his mouth, signaling silence. Mya stopped, immediately followed by the rest of the group. None of them moved; they only listened. Mya could hear the whistling of the wind and the sound of her own breath, but nothing else.

"Something is coming," said Quixitix. "Be ready."

The group stood stone still, waiting. Mya unlocked the Fabricant inside her and was preparing to create something to fend off whatever Quixitix had heard. The next sound was a scream and Mya knew she was already too late.

With the speed of the wind, Lucious was snatched from the spot on which he stood. He let out a scream, only one, but it was loud enough to alert his companions. The travelers all spun in different directions looking for the source of Lucious' peril but saw nothing, their clothing and scarves billowing in the cold wind swirling around them.

"Lucious! Quixitix, Dunny what is it?" shouted Mya.

"I don't know! Where is he?"

They could see nothing around them, but Lucious was gone. They heard a sound, guttural and savage, rumbling from the East.

"This way!" shouted Mya. They raced through the snow, following the sound. Moments later they found themselves facing a large outcropping of trees, white tipped and covered in snow like candy.

"In here," said Mya, then she spoke the Word. A faint light began to glimmer around the group. "Make sure you stay within this pocket. It should protect you." Lavinia nodded along with Quixitix and Dunny. They entered the forest.

It only took them a few steps before the attack began. From the trees swooped creatures none of them had ever seen before, ghastly hybrids of animals from the forest. The creatures made sounds no natural beast had ever uttered and as they came at the group surrounded by Mya's protective light, Quixitix drew a large blade from the folds of his robes.

"Dunny, move!" shouted the old professor. His brother did as he was told, although slowly and with some lethargy, but it was good enough. A flying combination of what looked like a fox and a bat screeched toward the glimmering barrier. From within it, and at just the right moment, Quixitix thrust his blade forward. The blade struck the animal with an audible piercing sound and it fell to the ground, warm blood melting the soft, white snow. From all sides different creatures, some with fangs, some with tails, and some with parts no one recognized, attacked the group. A white snow owl, spinning its head from side to side, swooped down upon them with the body of a hawk. From the trees a bear appeared with a snake for its head. More and more of these terrible chimeras appeared as Mya tried to protect her friends with the barrier of light. Each time one of the twisted creatures would attack, the barrier would shine and deflect the beast, sending it away with a terrible scream. When he could, Quixitix would thrust his knife through the barrier and connect with one of the attacking monsters; Mya doing her best to sync her control of the barrier with the attacks from Quixitix' knife. Lavinia cowered in the center of the group and Mya did the best she could to keep them moving toward the sound of Lucious' voice. Eventually the attack from the beasts wained and the group moved further into the trees.

"This way," said Mya above the yells of the creatures.

She led them forward, slowly. There was a small path cut into the trees and Mya noticed it first. "In there," she said and pointed toward the passage.

"Dunny won't be able to fit through there Mya," said Quixtix, slashing at another oncoming animal and missing.

"It's okay; you three stay here and just give me some time. I will find Lucious."

"Be careful Mya. You don't know what Allcraft has in there," said Quixitix.

"Allcraft? You think he is behind this?"

"Absolutely. These creatures are just like the Bargouls. Not as complex," Quixitix slashed again, connected and drawing blood from a squirrel and hawk combination, "but the same dark force created them.

"I'll be careful," said Mya, entering the small tunnel in trees.

The ground was cold and hard and Mya had to crawl to make it through the tunnel. The sound of the attacking creatures began to fade as she progressed and the thick canopy overhead began to block out the light. She spoke the Word and a small ball of light appeared above her shoulder and hovered there. She could see the end of the tunnel now and as she moved toward it she thought she heard faint breathing coming from the other end.

She emerged into a small clearing. A thickly knotted system of trees created a rooftop above her and there was no light save for her glowing orb. Lucious was curled up on the opposite side of the clearing, breathing very heavily.

"Lucious, are you alright?" asked Mya. He did not respond.

Mya made her way toward him and noticed for the first time how old he looked. She had no idea where the thought came from but in the strange fortress of trees crawling on the cold ground she suddenly could not help but notice how much the boy had aged. The thought flashed and was gone as quickly as it had come.

"Lucious, it's going to be okay, I'm here. Come on."

Lucious sat, frozen, terrified and staring, just over Mya's shoulder. Mya noticed the stare before she heard the sound.

"You . . . . must be the one he told me about." The voice hissed and changed strangely in pitch as it spoke, sending a gruesome chill through Mya. She didn't want to turn around but she knew she had to.

Moving toward Lucious and spinning at the same time, Mya turned and prepared herself for whatever sort of creature the voice belonged to. She did not prepare enough and when she saw it, let out a gasp.

"Are . . . you afraid?" The thing hovered above them, black and sinewy, its stiletto legs pointed and sticking to the trees above. Mya knew exactly what type of creature Allcraft had used to create this and she watched as eight identical dark legs jittered and danced, clicking like raindrops on the trees as it moved toward them.

"He . . . told me . . . you would come . . . he gave me . . . voice and thought . . . . to tell you something."

Mya could barely make out the face of the thing and she wasn't even sure if it was a face at all. It had millions of eyes, moving in the darkness above, watching them, and her small ball of light only helped to amplify the terror of this massive creature. The aroma it gave off reminded Mya of the kitchen she would sneak into as a child; rotting meat and sweat.

"Tell . . . me what?" stuttered Mya.

"Tell you about . . . your brother . . . about the Magican."

"What has Allcraft done to him? Is he here; is he here at the Loam?" At the mention of Michael some of Mya's courage returned.

"I do not know . . . what the Loam is. But your brother is gone to you . . . I was told to tell you to let him go . . . he wants nothing to do with you anymore . . ." The strange rise and fall of the voice disturbed Mya greatly.

"I don't care what Allcraft says. I am going to find Michael. And I am leaving here with this boy," said Mya, tilting her head toward Lucious.

"But I want that one . . ."

With blinding speed, the spider struck with its jet black leg, shooting it toward Mya. She felt it whiz past her head and strike the tree behind her, just barely missing both of them. Quickly, she spoke the Word and a wall of flame appeared between Mya and the spider. The creature recoiled, and moved upward toward the canopy. Although the wall of fire kept the spider at bay, it also blocked the only passage leading out of the small clearing.

"He told me . . . that I could kill you . . ."

"Well I'm so sorry to disappoint you," said Mya.

The spider could not see the two small things beyond the blinding wall. It did not understand or know what fire was exactly, but it could sense the danger from it and so it waited patiently in the canopy for its prey. After a few moments, the wall of fire receded. It waited; motionless, legs ready to strike as soon as it saw the small things move. And then it did; from the shadows it saw them dash forward. Instinct took over and, in one brilliant motion, the spider shot two of its legs toward them. The legs struck true, piercing the small creatures through the chest. The feeling was utterly satisfying to the spider and it let out a small sound of ecstasy. It lifted its prey up to the canopy, glad and filled with joy. The creature could feel the weight of newly caught prey on its legs; it felt good. Then it noticed something else, a sound, but was distracted with victory and did not pay attention. Instinct again took over and the spider began to wrap its prey in webbing, unmindful of the fact that the small creatures he now held possessed no features of any kind. The spider did not understand this and ignored it, going about the work instead, hungry and anticipating.

"How long has she been in there?" asked Quixitix, raising his blade to fend off the attack of some kind of flying caterpillar.

"Not long," replied Dunny. He was also defending from an incoming creature and Dunny, with his massive hands, was able to grab the thing right out of the air and slam it to the ground.

"Lavinia, are you okay?" said Quixitix. The girl nodded and Quixitix saw her from the corner of his eye, but she said nothing.

"Do you think she's alright?" said Quixitix.

"I'm fine . . . we're fine."

Mya emerged from the hedge holding Lucious by the hand. The boy was muddied and his hair was tussled. His face looked terrified but he said nothing.

"Mya, thank the Seraphim," said Dunny.

"We have to get out of here. We need to get to the Loam and find Michael. Allcraft did this, left this here for us. He knows we are coming." Mya said all of this as fast as she could and motioned for the group to retreat from the snowy forest.

"What happened in there Mya?" asked Lavinia in a timid and tiny voice.

"It's okay Lavinia. Your brother is fine. There was a creature but we managed to escape."

"A creature?"

"Yes, one that I won't be able to forget for some time I imagine," she said, conjuring the image of that grotesque spider hybrid coming at her, eyes glistening, fangs dripping with the thought of her death. She wondered if the thing had yet realized the prey it so easily caught was only a Fabrication. "Come on, this way," said Mya, turning away from the tree grove.

Mya led the group back down the path they had come and back onto the main road. On the horizon, the Loam rose toward the grey sky like a sentinel, waiting for them.

"We have to be more careful. Allcraft could have more surprises for us," said Mya.

"Agreed. Children, stay behind Dunny at all times, alright?" cautioned Quixitix. Lucious and Lavinia nodded, empty and morose.

"Let's go. Michael needs us." Tossing back her long, curly hair Mya started forward, her footsteps crunching above the hard packed snow.

▼

CHAMBER OF THE SERAPHIM

"Your sister is coming." The voice, heard so often for so long now, did not affect Michael as it had in the past. This voice was now something that was just there, lingering around him; inconsequential. He could remember fearing the voice and the creature to whom it was attached but now . . . it was more like pity.

"Did you hear me? She is coming here. We must finish soon," said Bartlebug.

"I know what we must do Bargoul," replied Michael. His eyes were sunken and deep. Sleep, something he sorely longed for, something he had taken for granted as a child, was only a stranger to him now. He wished only to sleep like a normal person; without the waking, without the dreams and the nightmares, to just fall into a soft bed at night and fade into the blissful ether of that dream-sea. He brushed his long, black hair from his forehead and tucked it behind his ear.

"Then get on with it. You're the only one who can," smirked Bartlebug.

"I'm painfully aware of what I can and cannot do. You remind me of it so often . . ." said Michael, turning away from the Bargoul.

Michael stalked into the center of the chamber he occupied with Bartlebug. He was not sure where Lucas was at this moment, but his proximity was certain. The old Magican would not let Michael out of his sight; too important, too valuable. As he walked, he examined the marvels around him, the culmination of all the lies perpetrated by The Order of the Fabricantresses, by his mother, the manifestation of all that he once held sacred. The first few chambers were difficult for the boy to understand let alone be comfortable with. After the Cerulean School, Michael had no reason to trust Allcraft. But after months of traveling and seeing chamber after chamber, much like this one, Michael knew he could no longer deny the power of what Allcraft had shown him. Now, standing here at the top of the White Loam, Michael was surrounded by the Seraphim themselves, as he had been so many times over these last few years.

Allcraft had told him a great secret, a secret kept so imply guarded by The Order, that should it ever be told the world would never understand; a secret whispered to the boy as he floated above his family and friends in the Culling Chamber at the Cerulean School. The Seraphim were real, Allcraft had said. The Seraphim could grant the power of the Fabricant. The Seraphim were singing. There was more of course, but Michael needed to see it for himself. If nothing else he put himself in a position to keep watch on Allcraft, to stop him from hurting anyone else in Serafina. After so much time passed, two long years looking for Chambers, Michael imply accepted the reality of what he was doing. That seemed like a lifetime ago. Michael was different now. The truth opened his eyes.

"Well are you going to do it or not?" said Bartlebug. Michael found it difficult to adjust to being so close to the creature he had warred with for so long. It still disturbed him but he had grown numb to those feelings, like so many others.

"Settle down, Bartlebug," said Michael.

Slowly, Michael walked around the circular chamber, examining the inhabitants. Four of them were nestled here, buried for so long and hidden so well, no one ever imagined they existed. They became legend and dogma, gods either prayed to or feared. But they were certainly real. Michael laid his hand on one of the golden seats upon which one of the Seraphim had once sat, brushing his hand over the cold metal. The occupant had long since entered a state of decay and while the first few times were very difficult for Michael, it was not hard to look at the body now.

"Amazing how they are kept alive," said Michael.

"You say this every time, just get on with it," replied Bartlebug.

"It's just fascinating. How long do you think it took for their minds to go?"

Attached to the chair was a mechanism of some kind. Tubes, machinery, and various other plugs were fastened to the chair's occupant, covering her decayed face completely; a horrible mask, sinewy and tight. The most striking feature of this mask was the mouth piece; it was spread wide and huge, forcing the mouth of the mask's owner open to the sky above. This device led to another larger apparatus hanging above the room. Each of the four golden thrones had a similar device and all four connected to the central one. The machinery gave off a subtle buzzing sound, alerting Michael that it still functioned. This scene often haunted Michael's dreams but it gave him some comfort knowing he was helping these poor creatures, putting them out of their misery and allowing them to be free, just like Allcraft had said. This was important work, unraveling the lies The Order had perpetrated for so long, helping these slaves find the peace of death at last. And all this suffering for what? Allcraft had made that perfectly clear; control. The

Seraphim controlled the Twinning, channeling it into the women The Order selected for recruitment and preventing any male from ever acquiring the power of The Order. This is how they maintained power. This is why they murdered any male born with the power, special children outside their control. This was the truth Michael Smith had, for two years, worked to bring to light.

"Do you think these were the first Bartlebug? Do you think the stories are true about the White Loam? Lucas told me; the source of all life. Do you think these four are the original Seraphim? The first people to tap into The Twinning?"

"Does it really matter? Just get on with it so we can leave this place. You know the noise bothers me so."

Michael smiled. This had been so hard before, doing all of this. It had taken him months to understand and accept what Lucas was planning, the truth that Allcraft was trying to unveil for him. He had long since decided he was doing the right thing and everytime he peeled back the lies, he felt better. After all, the noise never really bothered him as it did Bartlebug.

Each of the Seraphim wore a golden mask. It covered their once beautiful faces entirely and extended down to the throat where it wrapped around like a golden rattlesnake. The mouths of the masks were open and, although Michael had never looked beneath one in all this time, he assumed the mouth of the Seraphim was open as well. From these mouths eminated a song; the Song of the Seraphim. A sound, a noise really, sustained and endless. It was the Word, constantly pouring from the throat of these women as it had been for ages before. The machines made sure of that.

The one next to Michael looked just like the others. He placed his hand on the forehead of the mask she wore and could feel the vibrations of the machinery and the woman's voice. Michael closed his eyes. A feeling came over him, something he was so used to now, something he had first experienced when he was just a boy sitting in a bathroom stall. He shifted but not all the way. He did not want to travel to Earth this time but only in between. Perhaps it was Twilight, perhaps not; Michael really wan't sure. He opened his eyes and saw the form of Bartlebug fade away. The Bargoul could not make this particular trip; only Michael could. He looked down. Just above his hand, in the center of the golden helmet which also existed in this place, a small jewel appeared. They were always different colors and Michael often felt himself looking forward to seeing what strand of the rainbow would come next. This one was a deep blue. He placed his hand over the dazzling jewel and felt it respond to his touch; growing warm. Plucking the jewel from the helmet, Michael held it in his hand and then let it drop to the floor. The sound of the crystal hitting the stone rang out above the Song of the Seraphim. Seconds later, the jewel vanished as a stream of blue light flowed up and around Michael. Then he shifted back.

"Welcome back Smith," said Bartlebug, who had watched Michael disappear seconds before.

"This one is finished," said Michael. Indeed, the voice eminating from this chair's occupant had ceased and Michael watched, as he had so many times before, the body of the Seraphim fade away into nothing. Seconds later the chair was empty and the metallic mask fell to the floor.

"Three to go," said Bartlebug.

Michael looked at the bee-creature and nodded.

He was doing the right thing. He was certain of that.

CHAPTER 4

▼

IN THE WHITE LOAM

The air hung heavy, dark and cold as the group entered the White Loam. As they moved into the massive stone entry way, the whistling of the snow storm receded and the sound of the company's footfalls began echoing inside the hall. Inside was very different from what Mya had expected. The stories and legends all told of a place full of life and beauty, a place of creation and peace. The room they now occupied did not fit this description. Dark walls and cold stone floors replaced the soft and soothing images Mya had grown up with. Tattered shades and ancient, long decayed artifacts filled the room. She noticed several stone structures, now only piles of debris. A massive carpet had once marked the path further into the structure, but now only ripped tatters remained. Candlesticks, weapons, paintings; Mya saw all of these things, familiar decorations from her childhood, littered about the entrance.

"What was this place? I mean, when it was used. Did people live here?" asked Mya.

"Doubtful," replied Quixitix. "I imagine it was a meeting place of sorts, perhaps some kind of place of study for the Fabricantresses. It seems so ancient . . ." he trailed off.

"Gives me the willies," said Dunny, looking around the room. His loud footfalls reverberated off the floor and bounced around the empty space as they walked.

"Lucious, Lavinia, are you alright?" asked Mya. The children nodded weakly and simply stared forward, oblivious to the cold and dark of the Loam. The smell of decay and cold, wet stone rose up to meet them and Mya thought she could smell something else in the stagnant air; like damp fur.

"Light," spoke Mya, the Word issuing from her throat. A small, floating aura of light appeared over her shoulder and illuminated the massive foyer.

The room was mostly barren and empty, signs of a civilization and people long since abandoned and forgotten. Half-chewed bones and other remains were scattered about the place, obviously a nesting ground for creatures of all sorts. In the back a huge staircase spiraled upward, a never ending skyward curve, inviting and terrifying at the same time.

"Up there I presume," said Quixitix, making a statement more than asking a question.

"Yes. They're here. Allcraft, and my brother. We won't be too late this time," replied Mya.

Dunny and Quixitix nodded, following Mya toward the staircase. Before they reached the first step a booming voice stopped them.

"You cannot enter here!" shouted the voice, shaking the walls and floor with its din. From the darkness all around them the air seemed to coalesce and come together, swirling and moving in all directions.

"I have seen this before, just stay still," yelled Mya.

"Alright," replied Quixitx and Dunny.

The shadow creature sprang to life in front of them and Mya realized this one was much more alive than the one she had seen in the room in the desert canyon.

"You cannot enter the realm of the Seraphim," boomed the voice.

"What are you?" shouted Mya in reply. Lucious and Lavinia cowerded behind Dunny and the giant did his best to protect them with his massive carriage.

"I am the guardian of the Seraphim. Only the chosen may seek the Seraphim. You are not one of the chosen. Leave, or perish."

"We have to see them," said Mya. "My brother, Michael, is there. I must see him, I must save him. Please, you must understand . . ." she was cut off.

"Leave, or perish. This is the Mandate of the Seraphim."

Mya could see the creature rearing up and growing in size, massive dark shadows swirling into shapes like claws and fiercesome eyes; Mya was certain it would attack at any moment. She gestured for Dunny and Quixtix to back up and they slowly crept away.

"Please, please hear me. The world is in danger, the Magicans are going to return, Lucas Allcraft is going to return and . . ."

"You speak of the chosen."

Mya paused, shocked.

"Lucas Allcraft is a chosen?"

"I will not answer your questions. Leave or perish."

Mya stood her ground, testing the creature to see what it would do. Suddenly it let out a piercing, wincing sound, and Mya knew the attack was imminent. She barely had time to react before the shadow creature shot toward her, a streak of black shadow. What happened next happened purely through instinct.

She did not even speak the word, she didn't have time, but from somewhere deep within the Fabricant heard her calling and the Shield of the Seraphim materialized before her as it had done when she needed it so many times before. The creature screamed and slammed into the glowing white barrier, so bright the room filled with white, calming light and Mya heard the shadow monster scream, not really a sound of pain but of surprise.

"You are one of the chosen. You may enter, Seraphim."

The creature disappeared back into the darkness of the shadows and the shield faded away. Mya, breathing heavily, stood and waited to see if the monster would come back. After a few moments of silence, she turned her back on the staircase to check on her companions.

"Everyone alright?"

They all nodded.

"What was that thing," asked Lavinia.

"I don't know Lavinia. I'm just glad it's gone now."

"Likewise," said Quixtix. "Mya, did it call you a . . ."

"Yes, it called me a Seraphim."

"What does that mean?"

"I don't know and right now I really don't care. I just have to find Michael."

Mya started forward again, toward the stairs.

"And what happens when we find him Mya?" asked Lucious from behind Dunny.

Mya turned toward the young man, who even in this darkness had very handsome features, and looked at him sternly.

"We bring him home," she said and began climbing the looming, cold stairs.

CHAPTER 5

THE TRUTH AT LAST

"Finished?"

"Just one more," replied Michael. Lucas Allcraft swept into the chamber of the Seraphim darkly, his long hair swirling around him as he moved across the floor.

"Good. We need to move on."

"Fine," said Michael. Bartlebug hovered quietly near the room's only window, staring out at the snow covered landscape. Glancing back, he saw Michael disappear, his corporeal body slowly fading away as he moved into the realm protecting the Seraphim. A few seconds later he materialized again.

"That's the last one. These are finished," said Michael, as the golden machinery crashed to the floor and another Seraphim faded from existence.

"Let's go then." Allcraft motioned for them to follow and glancing toward the entrance of the room, Allcraft stopped. His face contorted into a scowl of anger as he observed Michael's troublesome sister and her compatriots. They had lingered too long and she had finally caught up with them.

Michael saw them moments after Allcraft, unsurprised. He scanned himself for a moment, trying to find what the sight of his sister and his old friends might conjure in him. She had grown over these last two years; no longer the innocent young girl from the rose field. Her hair, longer, still fell in dirty and chaotic curls about her shoulders. He smiled at her, weakly.

"Michael," said Mya, standing in the doorway to the chamber. She was calm. Her brother looked so different; his hair, long and dark, midnight black; his face, pale and sunken. He looked as though he had not slept since last they were together. She saw something in his eyes as he stared at her; something familiar.

"Hello Mya. It has been some time," said Michael.

"You're right," said Mya.

Michael lingered on the thought of how much older his sister looked, her hair longer, her eyes deeper and filled with the weight of so many things.

"You look older Michael," said Mya, as though mimicking his own thoughts.

"I know," said Michael.

"Enough. I don't know what you are doing here Fabricantress, but we are leaving," said Allcraft.

"No. Michael is coming with us." As Mya said this, Quixitix and Dunny appeared from the shadows of the hallway.

When he saw them, Michael felt a small twinge of regret and sadness. He had given up these friends to set out on his crusade with Allcraft . . . did he miss them?

"I can't come with you Mya. You don't understand. What we are doing here . . ." Michael gestured, bringing Mya's attention to the now empty seats in the chamber, "what we are doing here will open everyone's eyes to the truth."

"The truth Michael? The truth is that you turned your back on everyone that loves you and even though you gave up on us, I never gave up on you. I've been looking for you ever since that night at the Cerulean School. Please Michael, just listen to me, just give me a chance . . ." Her palpable anger rose like a flame inside her; she had not realized how angry she was with him until he was standing here before her, in the flesh, for the first time in two years.

"Mya, it doesn't matter!" shouted Michael, his voice rising. As Michael spoke, Allcraft slowly began to edge his way toward the side wall where Bartlebug now hovered, silent.

"*What* doesn't matter Michael?"

"Mya, you don't understand . . . these seats were, just moments ago, occupied by the Seraphim."

Mya could see the struggle in her brother's eyes; she could see whatever truth he had discovered was eating away at him, pulling him down like gravity.

"Mya, the Seraphim are real and they are suffering. Allcraft showed me how to help them, how to put an end to their misery. This is the truth of the Fabricantresses. These suffering women, locked in these chambers . . . singing."

"Singing, what do you mean Michael?"

"We have found so many chambers like this . . . filled with slaves Mya, slaves of the Fabricantresses. They have been here since the beginning, siphoning the power of the Twinning, channeling it to the Order to make them more powerful, to give them the power they needed to rule Serafina, hoarding it for themselves and no one else."

"Impossible. The Seraphim are just a myth . . ."

"No Mya. They are real. We have been helping them this whole time," he gestured with his arms around the room, "helping them be free. Helping to stop what they have been doing, stop the infanticide and the tyrannical rule. Allcraft showed me everything."

"Michael, no! This can't be true. How can you trust him?" said Mya, nodding toward Allcraft who was now much closer to the wall.

"I didn't at first. But I had to see for myself. There are hundreds of chambers just like this; sick vestiges of a time long ago. These people have been kept alive by these machines, their voices filtering into the ether between the worlds, drawing on its power, funneling it back to the order, keeping their power alive. Even you have been given their power Mya. I'm sorry, but it has to end. What the Order has been allowed to do all these years . . . I have to stop it Mya."

Mya, speechless, looked at her brother.

"Michael, please . . . I need you."

Michael's head bowed, his eyes searching the floor.

"I'm sorry, Mya. I have to finish this work . . ."

"No Michael. You have to come with me, with us. We can help you, please . . ."

Michael looked up at his sister across the room, searching for answers in her face. Confusion filled Michael's mind.

"The Fabricant is more powerful than you ever imagined Mya," said Michael. "I can use it now. Another lie, perpetuated by the Order, to maintain power."

Mya watched as Michael searched for a solution, searched for a path to take, for an answer to the questions Allcraft had planted in his mind.

"Well, I suppose you are half right Michael." From the side of the room Allcraft, long silent, spoke. "I suppose there is no point continuing this little charade. Clearly you are going to go back with them. It doesn't matter anymore. The work you have done . . . is significant."

"What are you talking about Allcraft?" said Michael.

"You have been ending the suffering of the Seraphim, this much is true. But you have also been slowly ending the suffering of Earth as well." The light of the room danced across Allcraft's face, sending strange shadows at odd angles and darkening his features.

"What is that supposed to mean?" shouted Michael.

"Don't you see? Don't you see where we are? The White Loam? The mythical source of all life?" Allcraft let out a small laugh.

"What are you saying Allcraft?" demanded Mya.

"This is the first of these chambers, the progenitor, the original. From here, the Seraphim spread and created numerous others. We have dealt with many of them but here is where it all began, where all life began."

"That's impossible Allcraft, all life on Serafina couldn't have started here . . ." said Mya.

"Not life on Serafina darling," said Allcraft, moving a bit closer to Mya, "life on Earth."

Michael and Mya stood speechless trying to understand what Allcraft had just said.

"Don't look so baffled. Did you really think twin worlds just happened? Did you really think it was some kind of cosmic accident? No. The Seraphim created Earth, a Fabrication, a mere expression of imagination. Your world, Michael Smith, is nothing more than the culmination of thousands of songs, sung by the Seraphim; the ultimate expression of their power and the disgusting edifice of their avarice. So now you know the truth. Thank you for all the help though," said Allcraft, smiling.

"Impossible. No one is that powerful," said Mya.

"You're right. That is why there are hundreds of them, all singing in unison, their combined voices breathing life into all the ends of the Earth. Imagine it, a world, an entire world, created from imagination. I want that power. Hence why I needed your brother, and his unique abilities."

Michael, stunned, betrayed, his world crumbling, stood speechless.

"Why? You told me we were helping them!" said Michael.

"And you believed me. Earth is dying Michael, your world, and you are the reason."

"No. No, it can't . . . Earth can't be just a Fabrication, it's impossible . . . that is my home . . ."

"Michael, Michael look at me," said Mya from across the room. Michael looked up, eyes shaking and afraid.

"Come with us Michael," said Mya. She extended her hand, reaching for him. Michael looked at her and for a moment, perhaps it was the dim light, Michael saw his mother. It had been so long since he thought of her. His mind filled with an image of her, sitting on a bed, light from an adjacent window pouring onto her face.

"Mya, I will . . ." Before Michael could finish his sentence Allcraft acted.

From the side of the room where Allcraft now stood, a sheet of electric blue fire shot toward Mya's outstretched hand, accompanied by a visceral growl from Allcraft. Mya had no time to react. Michael watched everything. His sister tried to summon the shield but the fire was too fast and instantly her hand and arm were ablaze and she was screaming, agonizing wails from Allcraft's blue Magican fire.

"Mya, no!" shouted Michael, running toward her. At the same instant, Allcraft grabbed Bartlebug in his arms and ran toward the window at the far side of the chamber. Looking back only once at the burning girl and her traitorous brother, Allcraft jumped from the balcony and immediately soared into the icy air, flying under a grey sky toward a dark horizon. His dark form vanished on the horizon.

Quixtix and Dunny ran toward Mya, attempting to douse the fire burning through her meager clothes, but these were no ordinary flames and they could not be extinguished with fanning. Mya screamed as the fire licked her delicate skin.

"Mya!" Michael now stood in front of her and reacted with pure instinct.

"Water!" he shouted, the Word echoing through the chamber. A stream of water appeared from nowhere and splashed against Mya's arm. She was still screaming, and now the occupants of the room could begin to smell something burning, something alive. Mya threw her arm up and down in the air, trying to extinguish the fire. The water did nothing.

"Mya, Mya!" shouted Michael, "Hold on!"

Michael felt the Magicant rush inside him, flowing like a river, cascading like a waterfall. He extended his hands and from them jets of pure water flowed, poured all over the fire Lucas Allcraft had hurt Mya with. This seemed to work. Magicant versus Magicant. At last, the fire ceased and Mya collapsed onto the floor. Her hand and most of her arm was burned very badly. Some spots were worse than others. Michael could smell the distinct odor of singed hair. His sister lay in his arms, panting.

"Mya, can you hear me?" said Michael. She nodded, but did not respond. "We are going to help you, just hang in there."

"Quixtix, do you have any medical supplies?" asked Michael.

"Some, but not for this," said Quixitix.

"Give me what you have."

From his robes Quixtix produced some bandages.

"Tell me about the medicine used here for burns. Every detail," said Michael.

Quixitix did as he was told. He described the herb, found in nearly every province of Serafina, which is harvested and then made into a paste. Michael listened intently, forming a picture of the salve in his mind.

He spoke the Word and held out his hand. A small canister materialized in Michael's palm.

"Amazing," whispered Quixitix. He had never seen a male use the Fabricant.

"I don't know if this is even going to work, but it's worth a try," said Michael.

Dunny watched, helplessly, from the archway of the room as Michael attempted to heal his sister's burns. From the hallway, Lucious and Lavinia stared into the room, expressionless.

"Hold on Mya," said Michael. He spread the salve onto her wounds. Mya winced from the pain, nearly unconscious. Once the cream was applied Michael wrapped her arm with the bandages; her skin was red and raw from Allcraft's attack.

"Just rest Mya, just rest." Michael laid her head gently on the floor.

"It's good to see you all again," said Michael after Mya had fallen asleep. Quixitix and Dunny hesitated a moment, betrayal and indignation running through them.

"Likewise. Although we don't really approve of your leaving like that," said Quixitix.

"Yup. I've missed ya' Michael. Hasn't really been the same without ya," said Dunny.

"I know. I'm sorry." It was all he could say. There was so much to apologize for and Michael was still reeling from what Allcraft had said.

"Apparently so. It would seem you have been working to destroy an entire world," said Quixitix. Michael looked at him fiercely.

"I didn't know. I just didn't know. I'm sorry." His expression, pain and confusion, and the trembling of his hands as he carefully applied the newly created salve to his sister's wounds confirmed his conviction.

"You know now," said Quixitix. "And there is still time to set this right. It is still unbelievable what Allcraft said, about the Seraphim creating and sustaining your world, but your actions over the past two years could very well explain all of the soft spots we have been seeing. The fabric between worlds is weakening."

Mya winced, loudly.

"It's okay Mya," said Michael, ignoring Quixitix for the moment. He stood up. "Quixitix, would you mind watching her for a moment?" The old professor nodded and cradled Mya in his arms.

"Thank you," she managed.

Michael gazed at Lucious and Lavinia cowering in the hallway of the Seraphim chamber, squatting in the corner holding each other. These two lives, taken so casually; they remained a constant and terrible symbol of innocent suffering in the war of the Twinning. As he walked over to them, Michael placed a firm hand on Dunny's shoulder and glanced at the massive creature with a look of familiarity and a half smile. Dunny returned the glance.

"Hello again," he said to the twins. They did not respond, only stared at him. "You have been through so much and I am sorry what he did to you . . . what he stole from you. I have carried you both with me every day I was with him and not a moment went by that I didn't think of you and try to help you."

Still the twins stared blankly at Michael, eyes wide.

"I have seen a great deal traveling with Allcraft and he has shown me many things. He is very alluring in that way. I cannot give you back your Embers."

Michael, reaching out his hands, motioned for the twins to take his outstretched palm.

"Please, take my hands," he said. "This will help."

Cautiously, Lucious and Lavinia stood up and took Michael's hands, forming a circle of three. Michael closed his eyes for a moment. Quixitix and Dunny watched as a slow, pulsing light dimly began to illuminate Michael's form. The light seemed to rise and fall like a wave and soon the light began to move toward Lucious and Lavinia. The twins looked alarmed but continued to hold Michael's hands as the light began to engulf them. The colors subtly changed as the light moved across their bodies, blue, red, green and white. Eventually the light left Michael and lingered on the twins, then vanished.

Breathing heavily, Michael opened his eyes.

"How do you feel now?" he asked them.

Lucious blinked, several times, very quickly.

"I feel . . . I feel okay," he said.

Quixitix and Dunny were surprised to hear his voice, a sound they so seldom heard.

"And you Lavinia?" asked Michael. She looked up at him, her eyes a deep green, a green so brilliant they almost shone in the darkness of the Loam chamber. Michael could not help but feel pulled into that green expanse.

"Good. More normal . . . more, filled up."

"Good," said Michael. "This feeling will not last, not until we take back what Allcraft took from you. And I promise, we will find a way to do that."

The twins nodded and walked over to where Mya rested with Quixitix.

"I know where Allcraft will go next, if he sticks to his plan, which at this point might only be wishful thinking," said Michael, turning to face his companions.

"Where is he going?" asked Dunny.

"Without me, he will not be able to shift into the realm where the unprotected Seraphim rest. He needed me for that. I am unique . . . he often told me that," said Michael, looking at the ground. "So now that he no longer has a method to destroy the Seraphim he will most likely seek another way. He talked about it often. A book."

"A book?" asked Quixitix.

"Yes. Ancient, secret. You should have seen Allcraft's face when he would talk about it. He will seek it out and, eventually, he will find it. We have to find it first."

Mya opened her eyes, her breath heavy.

"Michael . . ." she said.

"Yes Mya?"

"The book. What is it called?"

Michael looked around at all of them, his long, dark hair falling about his shoulders in messy tangles.

"The Song of the Seraphim."

Mya smiled, weakly.

"We have to go see our mother Michael, before it is too late."

Michael thought for a moment, conflicted.

"Yes. I want to see her . . . I need to see her."

"She's sick Michael," said Mya.

"Sick? What do you mean?"

"She's dying Michael," replied Mya.

The weight of the news hit Michael in the pit of his stomach. His breathing became rapid and coarse and he could feel the tears welling in his eyes. He had felt such disdain and betrayal, such anger when he found out the truth about the Order and about what his mother had been a part of. As the words rolled off Mya's tongue Michael knew immediately all those feelings of pain did not matter and suddenly a memory burst into his mind like a bomb blast. He could see it so clearly; his mother and father cooking breakfast, the smell of eggs and the sound of the griddle flickering through the air. He was just a boy and on Saturday mornings they would all eat together; eggs, toast . . . the sun fell in through the kitchen window and made his mother shine, her hair vibrant in the sun's rays. He was so happy on Saturdays.

"Then we go see her. As soon as you are ready to move, we go right now."

"I'm ready," said Mya, standing up.

"We have a long trip back," said Quixitix.

"Not as long as you think," said Michael. "Everyone, hold hands."

They did as Michael instructed and formed a connected circle in the room.

"I've learned a few things these last years," said Michael, and smiled. Closing his eyes, he focused and the air around the room began to get hazy and strange.

"What's going on?" said Quixitix. As he watched, the air began to shimmer and soon grew transparent. Through this transparent air Quixitix could see something he knew to be impossible.

"That's my workshop . . . how in the world . . ."

"Step through the gateway," said Michael. "It's all about visualizing. If I have been there, if I can see it in my mind, there is a way to create a tunnel through Twilight straight to where you want to go. How do you think we were able to get to all these Seraphim chambers?"

"Incredible . . ." said Quixitix. Dunny stood silent and stunned like the rest of the company.

Quixitix was the first to break the circle and slowly approach the glimmering air. He could feel his hair tingling as he got closer. One cautious look back to Michael and then Quixitix entered the gateway and vanished. Seconds later, they could see a cloudy shape on the other side. One by one they all entered the gateway, Michael last. He looked one final time at the Seraphim chamber, prayed he would never see another one in his life, and vanished into the gateway.

DEPARTURE 4

LUCIOUS AND LAVINIA

The twin descendants of Lucas Allcraft, children born of Earth yet fatefully intertwined with the destiny of Serafina, stood motionless and silent under a massive oak tree. The tree's large and floppy leaves offered peaceful shade for the twins. In the summer breeze the leaves of the tree whispered to them. They both enjoyed that sound; they had enjoyed it on Earth as well as Serafina. Older now, the twins understood everything that had happened to them but that was all they could do. Lucious, unable to tell his sister how terrifying and painful it had been when Allcraft ripped his Ember away from his body, wanted nothing more than to reach out to his sister and offer her some kind of comfort, some kind of solace. Lavinia, her hair now streaked with white, a sign of the trauma and pain Allcraft caused her, wanted the same thing as her brother. Instead, they could only speak as though in a dream, like the distant and foggy call of ships in the night.

"I have never been to a funeral before," said Lucious. He simply stated a fact; his voice contained no feeling or emotion. Allcraft took those things from him. Lavinia simply nodded in reply.

"What do they call it here?" he asked her.

"Departure, I think," said Lavinia, her voice lifeless, her eyes empty and staring far beyond the ocean before them.

"Michael's father?" Lavinia nodded in response. "What are our parents doing, do you think?" The only reply Lucious received was a shrugged shoulder. The Departure of Peter Smith stirred up these thoughts for Lucious. Only weeks had passed since the events at the Cerulean School and during much of that time the twins had thought of their previous lives; their home, their family, their school . . . it all seemed a distant memory now, another life. Had they known the last, dying flames of their Embers would continue to fade as more time passed, they might have reflected even more about who they once were.

"They have taken care of us Lav," said Lucious, nodding to Dunny and Quixitix. "And Mya. They have taken good care of us." Again, he stated simple facts. He had forgotten how to feel.

"Yes, they have," replied Lavinia.

"And that man there, why is he dressed like that?" asked Lucious. His gaze traveled to the Orator overseeing the Departure. His formal gowns flowed about him in waves.

"I don't know. Some kind of priest or something I guess," said Lavinia in her soft, defeated voice.

Lucious looked around at all the people gathered on the hillside for the Departure. Some he knew and others he did not. He observed a family, a man and a woman with a son, approach Quixitix and Dunmire, shake their hands, and walk away. This family also spoke with Mya, only longer. Lillian stood as well, dressed all in white, by Peter Smith's empty casket. Lucious watched her face intently and he saw great sadness there. He wished for a moment he could feel sad for Peter, that he could feel something, anything again. He also saw several other families from the small town along the road leading to the cliffs. He imagined strangers paying him respect during his own funeral, wondered if he would approve of people he did not even know seeing him off after his death.

"Who is that?" said Lucious, pointing.

A figure cloaked in shadow appeared on the road, walking slowly over the last hill. Lucious had not noticed this person before.

"I don't know," said Lavinia. "I cannot see his face anyway."

Indeed, the shadowed head was down and a dark hood masked any features of a face.

"I think he's saying something," said Lucious, his attention moving away from the hooded figure and fixing upon the man with the large gown.

"Is he starting the ceremony?" asked Lavinia.

"I think so, come on," said Lucious. Taking Lavinia's hand, Lucious led her away from the tree and they found a spot in the crowd off to one side. Neither of them noticed the second figure, another stranger; suddenly appear on the road behind the figure in black.

"And so we join together, as one voice, as one heart, to send this loved one to eternal peace," said the Orator, addressing the crowd. As he spoke, Lucious and Lavinia watched Mya and Lillian standing at the front of the crowd, their eyes gazing down at the ornamented casket. Only once did Lucious glance back at the hooded stranger who had chosen to remain on the hilltop, watching the ceremony from a distance; the other stranger he did not see. Lucious looked at his sister, her pale skin and sunken eyes, and promised himself one day he would fix her, bring her peace like this Orator brought peace to these people. Lucious was aware the Orator had stopped talking but he continued watching Lavinia as she stared straight ahead with empty eyes. Then the twins, like everyone else gathered there, saw only darkness. They awoke the next day with memories only of the Departure, with empty souls and with the news that Queen Lillian VanVargott was ill.

CHAPTER 6

▼

LILLIAN'S GOODBYE

The massive twin windows of Lillian's room were closed now, the pale yellow drapes drawn taught. In the dim light of her chamber her bed seemed to cower in one corner of the room and the only sound, the faint ocean wind buffeting the cottage, filled the room with a dark noise.

"Mom. Mom, it's me," said Michael from across the room. His voice echoed along the alabaster walls, reverberating softly. He could hear the sound of his mother's pained breathing from where he stood, in and out, harsh and slow, and the wind against the windows outside.

"Michael," said Lillian, rasping. Michael could hear the strain in her speech, her attempts to make her voice, already so weak with disease, sound strong to her son. "It is so good to see you again. Come here." She motioned for him to come closer and he obeyed, moving across the large expanse of the room quickly. Michael's mind quietly conjured up an image, a memory, and presented it to him as he walked toward her; a bright morning, various drawings hung on walls, the smell of antiseptic and bandages. Michael remembered seeing his mother at that place. It felt like several lifetimes ago, a time and place so far removed from this moment Michael could barely recognize it. But still his mind persisted and showed him things; a hand drawn image of a large bee, the white sheets of her bed resting softly under the sunlight, the smell of cotton and peppermint, his mother sitting there, waiting for him.

"Michael," she said. He stood beside her and looked at her face. He thought about his choice, the one he made so long ago, it seemed. He remembered standing outside the Mayweather's home, yelling; screaming. Telling her how much he hated her. He recalled how those feelings swelled in him that night in the Culling Chamber, floating above the ground, face to face with Lucas Allcraft. He remembered how angry he had felt, how ashamed. He had wanted nothing but to prove his mother wrong, go off with Lucas Allcraft, rebel against everything she had ever done for him and show her the façade plastered in front of her.

"Mya tells me you can wield the Fabricant now?" Michael was surprised that this was the first thing she asked him after all this time.

"Yes. Lucas showed me it's possible. Another lie from the Order I guess," said Michael, instantly regretting his words.

"Indeed. Sometimes the truth must be hidden to protect the ones we love," said Lillian, her eyes, sunken yet still burning with life. "Sometimes, the truth is more painful than the lies."

"I guess," said Michael. "I don't think I believe that though." His voice was not angry; just resolved.

"I'm sorry for lying to you Michael. I'm sorry I never told you about the dark history of the Fabricantresses. But most of all . . ." she paused, catching her breath, "most of all I'm sorry if you feel I betrayed you."

"I never felt betrayed, not really. I just needed answers. Answers I knew you couldn't give me."

Lillian nodded and took a deep, labored breath.

"I know. I am glad for this," she said. "Glad you were able to find what you were looking for."

"But it has cost us," said Michael. "I understand that now. I never should have trusted Allcraft. It was all a game; lies to get me to do what he wanted."

"I know. So you really saw them then? The Seraphim?"

Michael nodded. "Yes. Wretched creatures now, kept alive so long. I felt sorry for them, felt like I was helping them. Putting them out of their misery."

The candle next to Lillian's bed flickered, casting long shadows along the walls. The wind picked up for a moment outside as mother and son spoke, the windows reverberating slightly against the battering of the sea breezes.

"I know. You thought you were doing the right thing."

"Instead I've put us all in jeopardy." He looked at his mother. "Is it too late?"

For a moment she did not answer, only looked at him, and smiled a small, wry smile with her dry lips.

"No," she said. "Do you miss your father?"

Michael was afraid of this question. He had tried not to think about his dad, tried to push the feelings aside. Had he known that night in the Culling Chamber everything would have been different . . . .

Lillian spoke, as if reading his mind, "you didn't know Michael. I'm glad you were at the Departure."

Surprise spread across Michael's face. "How did you know?"

"Do you remember what happened?" said Lillian, straining.

"I remember the Orator speaking. I remember seeing Mya, Dunny and Quixtix . . . the Mayweather's, Lucious, Lavinia. I remember seeing you cry."

"Is that all?" asked Lillian.

Michael thought for a moment, trying to remember. He could see the crowd standing by the cliff from the hillside on which he stood, his black robe concealing his face. He knew he had to be there but also knew he was not ready to return. Back then, his work had only just started and Allcraft's lies were still fresh in his mind. He saw the image of his father's casket, the ornamental seal of the Seraphim glistening in the . . .

"Do you remember now?" asked Lillian, coughing.

"They all fell down," said Michael quietly. How could he have forgotten this? How could his mind have omitted something so strange?

"They all fell down, and I watched them. All at the same moment," he looked up at his mother, "all of them except you."

"Yes," said Lillian. "I looked back at you on that hill. Looked into your eyes and I saw you were not ready yet. I could have stopped you then, perhaps. Perhaps not . . ."

"What are you talking about mom?" asked Michael.

"I had to hide it Michael. So he could never find it."

"Hide what?" The wind crashed against the building loudly.

"The Song of the Seraphim. The ancient text upon which the entire Order of the Fabricantress is built. It holds the secrets of this world . . . and of Earth. It tells of the White Loam, and the original women who discovered the power of the Twinning. How they tapped into that power. And how they became greedy." Lillian coughed, harder this time. Michael noticed her hands were shaking.

"If Allcraft possess this text he will inherit the power to destroy both worlds Michael. He will inherit the knowledge of the Seraphim, the original Fabricantresses, and he will desire nothing else but to create a new world in his image."

"Create a new world? What are you talking about?"

Lillian smiled. Reaching up, she touched her hand to her son's face, gently caressing his cheek. He looked so much older now, his long hair and rough skin, so much different than the boy she remembered.

"It is why you are so special Michael. I honestly did not even think it was possible. But you arrived; my miracle. A boy born of a world that does not exist. The perfect intersection of Serafina and Earth. You, Michael, are that miracle," she coughed again, harder. "This is why you are able to tap into both sides of the Twinning; why you can access Twilight, why it is up to you to save us all. Without you, Allcraft will kill all the Seraphim, stop them from proclaiming their song, and destroy the Fabrication that is Earth."

Michael had heard all of this before, from Allcraft at the White Loam.

"You knew about this? This whole time? From the very beginning?"

Lillian nodded. "I am a direct descendant of the Seraphim. It is my duty to protect this secret. I was selfish. I knew about Earth since I was a child, since the Fabricantresses first took me from my normal life, since the elephant . . ." she trailed off.

"Elephant?" said Michael.

"It does not matter now. All that matters is that book, Michael."

"The Song of the Seraphim?"

"Yes."

"Where is it then?" asked Michael.

"Hidden."

"What?"

Michael thought for a moment, his mind trying to put the pieces of this story together, to understand his mother's actions. Like shattering glass, it hit him.

"That's why you're sick," said Michael, very quietly. Lillian said nothing, her silence confirming his guess.

"You did that to them at the Departure, it was you."

Again, Lillian said nothing. Michael could see her eyes closing slightly, as though she wanted to sleep.

"Yes," she whispered. "I'm sorry Michael. I had to. I used everything I had left to strip the words from the book and put them somewhere else, a place filled with light . . . I put the words into a stone and that is in a place where only you can go. The book I hid back at the castle and the words I put in a Culling Stone. Do you remember your father's casket?"

"Yes, I only saw it from the hilltop but I remember it. Isn't it gone though? Sent off to sea?"

"Yes, but the stone . . ." said Lillian.

"What do you mean? I remember seeing the Orator . . ." he trailed off. What did he remember, exactly?

"I made you remember seeing the Orator send him off, made them all remember it. It was more than I could handle and now it has taken more from me than I thought it would. He is gone . . . his casket is gone but the Culling Stone . . ."

"Where's the stone Mom?" asked Michael. Lillian smiled.

"I hid it. Somewhere sacred and safe. A place where your father's memory will be," she coughed, and continued "held sacred forever. And the Song of the Seraphim will remain safe."

"Mom, please where is it?" Lillian closed her eyes, the lids flickering slightly. Just then, the door slowly opened and Mya appeared, her long hair falling upon her shoulders.

"Michael, are you . . ."

"Mya, come here, quickly," said Michael.

Running across the room, her footsteps echoing against the walls and mixing with the sound of the wind outside, Mya found herself next to her brother and staring into the closed eyes of her mother.

"Michael, is she alright?"

"Here," said Michael. He picked up his mother's hand and placed it into Mya's. She could feel the lightness of it and the dryness of her skin. She looked at Michael, his eyes intense and pained. Michael took her other hand in his.

"Mom," he said softly. "Mom, everything is okay. Mya's here."

"Mother," said Mya softly, putting Lillian's hand to her cheek.

"Children," said Lillian, her eyes closed, her mouth a tiny smile. "Children, you are both loved. Loved eternally," she whispered. The wind outside had stopped completely and the only sound in the room now was Lillian's shallow breathing.

"I love you mom," said Michael.

"Mother. I love you," said Mya.

They watched Lillian smile and listened until they heard nothing at all. Several silent moments passed; no breathing, no wind and then nothing but tears.

Chapter 7

▼

Clouds on the Horizon

"She has died."

"Indeed. And what of the book?"

"I do not know."

The speakers stood silhouetted against the dark backdrop of the evening sky. The first, Lucas Allcraft, pulsated with anger and hatred for the family standing in his way. He took some solace and joy in the fact that at least one of them, and a quite powerful one at that, was finally dead.

The other, a pathetic creature, his path through life twisting and turning and eventually bringing him to a place he could only understand through confusion, hovered beside his master.

"Bartlebug. You have served me so well all these years; centuries. You have lasted, persisted, through wars and struggle, through history, through countless years, alone." The Bargoul said nothing. The pride in his eyes white, pin-prick eyes was clear.

"And now we come to our most dire hour, old friend. You are the only one who has stood by me through all this," said Allcraft, waving his hand at the dark horizon, "and now we must see it through. The Fabricantresses promised me so much then, promised me a world of my own, a world created and ruled by me. Their betrayal still mocks me," he paused, staring into the darkness.

"Indeed Master Allcraft. Your revenge is at hand, at long last."

"Yes Bartlebug, but revenge is not enough. They must be stopped. The Order, the Fabricantresses, the entire thing. We need that book. We need the power of the Seraphim. Without it, I cannot forge my," he looked at his companion, "*our* world."

"Yes Master. We must find it. Is her's the only one that still exists?" Allcraft nodded. "Then we must find a way to discover its location."

"There is only one way. Can you still contact the rest of your Brotherhood?" said Allcraft, glancing down at the green marking on Bartlebug's hindquarters.

"Yes. What's left of them, anyway."

"Good. We will need a force, Bartlebug. As many as you can muster."

"Anything, Master Allcraft."

"We need Mya VanVargott. And we need that book."

On the horizon, a blue streak of electric lightning split the sky as the clouds of war gathered and drew close.

CHAPTER 8

▼

A GIFT FROM LONG AGO

The Departure of Lillian VanVargott, once Queen of the Kingdom of Blanchfield, lacked any of the ornate trappings of a typical royal departure. Only her family and friends attended, those she had loved and struggled with for so many years. Her son and her daughter stood before her casket and watched as Orators spoke, gestured, and sent her body away for peaceful, eternal rest. The memory of Peter Smith's Departure rested firmly in both their minds; Mya standing before the casket then just as she stood before one now, Michael observing from a faraway hilltop. They cried and consoled, they spoke words of reassurance and hope, words of love and kindness, yet everyone there felt a keen emptiness, a void that no words could fill. Michael and Mya, now orphans, parentless, could only console each other. Their childhood, a long past echo, something only felt and not remembered, was gone. As they watched their mother's casket drift toward the horizon they knew the only path was forward, toward a world without this kind of suffering, a world without menace and fear looming in the distance, looming like one great shadow over the minds of people who deserve only love and joy. They said goodbye and it was done.

Alone at last, the children of Lillian VanVargott, a woman once called Judith Smith, sat together in the upper room of Quixitix' old workshop on the outskirts of Aside. The place had not been kept up over the years and overgrowth, dust and decay covered most of the space. Downstairs, Michael and Mya could hear Quixitix fumbling around, beginning the work of making the place new again.

"Why did she send you to Blanchfield if she knew the book was empty?" asked Michael. Mya had told him the story of her journey home, her encounter with Krys in the castle, and the secret room kept hidden beneath her mother's chambers, a room filled with remnants of Earth.

"I don't know Michael." Mya's eyes were tired and swollen. Her hair, long and tangled, moved with her head.

"Unless she wanted you to find something else there. A clue perhaps?"

"Then why wouldn't she just tell me? Why all the tricks and games?" The anger in her voice was just at the surface. Michael understood. He was angry too but he could not focus on that now, not with Allcraft out there, somewhere.

"I know Mya, I understand your anger." Mya shot him a piercing look, those blue eyes glaring, eyes Michael had once thought beautiful in a rose field when he was just a boy. "But we have to focus on the book. We must find it before Allcraft . . . my world is being destroyed. Earth is going to die and I helped kill it. We cannot let Allcraft finish the job."

"Then let's go back to the castle. Let's go look together at mother's secret little room."

"Do you think we might find . . ."

"Well it's better than sitting here and talking about it!" shouted Mya, standing up. Without looking at her brother she stormed from the room and slammed the door. Michael sighed. He never wanted to hurt anyone.

"Angry, she is." The voice came from the shadows at the very edge of the small room, a dark crevice where the light from the candles did not reach. Michael jumped at the sound, thinking he was alone now that Mya had left.

"Who's there?" said Michael, standing. "Show yourself."

"Don't be afraid, Michael Smith. It has been a very long time since I have seen you. I thought perhaps one day you might return here and so here I be," said the voice. From the corner of the room Michael saw some movement in the shadows. His mind instantly summoned the Magicant, his fist becoming a ball of indigo flame, and he shone the light in the direction of the movement. At first his mind did not recognize the figure and then it came back to him, like a wave from the Emerald Ocean.

"Phillip," said Michael, his memory reaching far back and his mind conjuring an image of a Bargoul floating above the dusty sands of the Emerald Shores.

"Remember me now, do you?" said the Bargoul, illuminated by Michael's burning fist.

"I do." It was the WaveWatcher Michael had met when he had been sent away to Aside, the Bargoul who had stood watch on the beach. "You have been here this whole time?"

"Indeed. I don't follow the others. I don't follow Bartlebug. I saw it then, on that day. Just a shadow, I saw. Just a misty vision, something vague . . . but I knew you would be so important, so important so I had to wait for you."

Michael noticed how the Bargoul walked, slowly and as though in pain.

"The girl is angry."

"I know."

"I can help you. I can help you very much. Here," said the Bargoul. From a small pouch draped around his body the Bargoul produced a small piece of reflective glass. Michael knew this to be a mirror; here it was called Twin Glass.

"This will help you find what you seek."

"The book?" said Michael.

"Yes," said the Bargoul. "I knew her father you know."

"Who? Mya's father? King Charles?" The Bargoul nodded.

"I served him before Bartlebug came to the castle. I knew the Queen too. She gave me this when I was young."

Michael took the mirror from the Bargoul and examined it. He could see his own reflection staring back at him, his long black hair falling around his shoulders.

"What am I supposed to see?" asked Michael.

"I do not know, but I have gazed into the Twin Glass many times in my long life, times I felt lost, times I felt confused. It has helped me greatly." The Bargoul nodded, as one would after completing a task with great pride, and shuffled toward the door.

"Where are you going?"

"To the sea Michael. I want my last sight to be the Emerald Ocean."

"Your last sight?" The Bargoul looked back at Michael and Michael thought he saw a small smile creep into the creature's face.

"This world no longer has need of me and so I shall bid it farewell. Too much change, too much strife. I hope you can make a better world, one day."

With that, the old Bargoul opened the door and left the room, leaving Michael holding the mirror and wondering what, exactly, he should do with it. He glanced down at it again and still saw only his own face but . . . something else perhaps? He peered closer, staring into his own reflection, examining his face, much older now, his eyes, much harder now. He thought about how much he had changed, grown up, how different he was from his childhood self; just a boy in school worrying about bullies, about backpacks, about his parents splitting up, about his math homework. That life seemed so far away now. As he stared into the mirror he began to imagine himself as a boy, what he had looked like, what he had hoped for in life, what had given him joy and what had brought him sadness. The image in the mirror began to change, began to grow younger. Soon Michael was staring at himself, suddenly just a boy and there, in his hands, something so long forgotten, something cherished so long ago. As soon as he saw it he knew, he knew in that moment; he knew exactly where to go. He blinked and the image was gone, replaced by Michael's current reflection. He wondered if it had ever changed at all. It didn't matter. He rushed out of the room, stuffing the mirror into his pocket.

"Mya, Mya!" he shouted.

"Down here," responded Quixitix.

"Mya, we have to go now. I know where the book is."

From below, Michael saw Mya appear in the center of the room and look up at him. From the balcony he spoke and Mya listened.

"We need to go back to Blanchfield. The book is there."

"No it's not, I searched the entire . . ."

"Mya, it's there. Trust me. It has been there all along. I just forgot . . ." said Michael.

"Fine," said Mya. "Are you going to open one of those portal things again?"

Michael smiled. "Quixitix, we will be back shortly. Come on Mya."

Michael charged down the stairs and, taking Mya's hand, focused on his memory of Castle Blanchfield until the image was ripe in his mind. Slowly, a small portal opened in Quixitix' shop and the children of Lillian VanVargott stepped through, glancing back at Quixitix one last time. The old professor nodded, his bushy eyebrows hiding the fear looming like a storm cloud behind his eyes.

CHAPTER 9

▼

TREASURE ISLAND

"Again! Again!" shouted the young boy, his floppy brown hair hanging mop-like over his forehead. He smiled and curled himself up tighter; his blue pajamas with ducks splashing in pools all over them disappeared under the protection of his bedspread. "Again!" he said.

"The same one?" asked the woman.

"Yes."

"Are you sure? *Treasure Island* again?"

The boy nodded and watched his mother open, yet again, the Great Illustrated Classic *Treasure Island;* it was the boy's favorite book and he had heard it at least twenty times from his mother. He had started to read it on his own a little too.

"Chapter 1: Pieces of Eight," said the woman, glancing at her son from above the pages of the book. Her eyes, blue and piercing, always looked strangely wondrous to the boy; like eyes that had seen things he never would. The mother read the words on the page, lingering over certain ones, pausing at key moments, building up her son's excitement and then delivering an important line. The boy loved when his mother did this. He would dream of pirates and chests filled with gold doubloons, talking parrots and old Ben Gunn stranded on that island wishing only for his delicious cheese. He listened with the attention of a rapt and captivated audience; a literary prisoner held by the pirates in the pages.

"I think we should stop there for tonight," said the boy's mother.

Reluctantly, the boy accepted his mother's proposal under the express promise that more pirate adventures would continue the next night. The woman glanced around her son's room, as she always did each night. The ABC wallpaper, the wooden toy train set on his shelf, the drawing of the park he did in school complete with happily buzzing bumblebees hovering over the green bushes. She placed the book on the bedside table, the image of the swarthy pirate standing on the shores of Treasure Island staring up at her. She secretly loved this tale too; there was nothing like this where she came from.

"Peter, do you want to say goodnight to Michael?" she called.

"Of course," came the reply. From the hallway a tall man in glasses appeared wearing a green sweater over a white shirt.

"Did you enjoy the story, kiddo?" he said.

"Yea Dad. It's my favorite," replied Michael.

"I know. Goodnight son," said Peter walking to Michael and kissing his forehead.

"Night dad."

"Goodnight sweetheart," said the boy's mother, brushing his hair off his forehead. She reached over and with a familiar click turned off the bedside light.

"See you in the morning," came a voice from the dark.

"Definitely," said Peter. The boy's parents left the room and slowly closed the door. In the hallway they exchanged a quick kiss and a look that said how much they loved their son. As Peter walked away the woman thought of her other child, a child so far from her now and, perhaps, lost forever. Her little girl; how she missed her. Mya. The woman looked back at the door to her son's room and wished she could go back, somehow bring them together, somehow tell everyone she loved the truth. For now, all she could do was love the child she had and pray to the Seraphim her longing for Mya would not drive her mad.

CHAPTER 10

▼

RETURN TO CASTLE BLANCHFIELD

As they stepped through the portal Michael's mind still lingered on his memory of *Treasure Island* and his parents, happy, tucking him in at night. He wished for more memories like that one but the few he did have, he cherished.

"I bet you wish you could do this a long time ago," said Mya, stepping onto the hard ground.

"This portal thing? Yea, would have been a lot faster than that hot air balloon."

The scene around Michael and Mya was dark and barren yet so familiar to both of them. Michael had been to this particular place many times. In fact, this was the very first sight of Serafina he ever saw; that day when he shifted for the first time in the boy's bathroom at Levi.

"Light." The Word came from them nearly at the same time and they looked at each other in surprise as a small ball of light lifted from each of their hands and floated just above their heads.

"It's going to take me a while to get used to that," said Mya. "Why is it, again, that you can use the Fabricant?"

"I'm not sure Mya but that's what Lucas told me about above the Culling Chamber that night. He said it was just one of many lies the Order had perpetrated to maintain control, to maintain power. I think it has something to do with Mom and the fact that I am sort of half from here and half from Earth, if that makes any sense."

Mya shrugged. "Well, if it's true that Earth is just a giant Fabrication then I guess you are partly made from the Fabricant and . . ." Standing there in the dim light the realization of what Mya was saying washed over her like a crashing wave. The look of dismay on her face, clear to Michael, prompted him to speak first.

"I know," he said. "I have already thought about it."

"What will happen to you if Allcraft gets his way?" Mya nearly shouted.

"I don't know. If he destroys Earth, if he stops the Seraphim singing, then I guess everything that is part of that Fabrication would cease to exist. Even me."

"Michael . . . I can't lose you. I can't lose you, too," said Mya in the semi-darkness.

"Then we have to find that book and we have to stop him. I have already made so many mistakes."

"There's the castle," said Mya, pointing ahead. From the outside Castle Blanchfield looked dark and gloomy; a much different sight than the magnificent kingdom Michael had seen upon his second visit to Serafina.

"Do you really think it's in there?" asked Mya.

"I'm sure of it," said Michael. "Let's hurry."

Following the dimly glowing orbs floating above them, Michael and Mya rushed toward Mya's childhood home now just a graveyard for haunts and other creatures of shadow, a dim memory of a once great kingdom.

Chapter 11

A Dark Reunion

"I need that book."

His voice, cold, harsh and immensely furious, filled the room like spreading flame. Lucas Allcraft sat at the head of a long, wooden table. From the stone walls several torches flickered and cast strange shadows all around him. Seated at the table were several Bargouls of various sizes and colors and next to Allcraft sat Bartlebug.

"We have something that may help master," said Bartlebug. Allcraft scowled at him.

"And what might that be?"

"Bring her," shouted Bartlebug.

From the far corner of the room a few Bargouls, floating, shuffled a bound and gagged figure through the narrow archway.

"And who might this be?" said Allcraft, his voice rising slightly.

"We found her not far from here master. She claims to have information about the book."

"Unbind her," said Allcraft.

Floating up, one of the Bargouls removed the gag and the cover from the woman's face.

"Surprise, surprise. I am truly shocked," said Allcraft, sitting back in his chair and rubbing the sides of his mouth.

"Indeed," said Ja'Mirra. Her face, still not fully healed from Allcraft's attack in the Culling Chamber, glistened red.

"Why are you here Fabricantress? Do you not remember out last meeting? When I killed you?" said Allcraft, smiling.

"I do," replied Ja'Mirra.

"Then why help me now?"

"Because in the end my lust for power has overcome my desire for revenge. I want to help you create your new world. After all, I did work so hard to bring you back here. Think how much easier it will be with an actual Fabricantress by your side."

Allcraft's mind quickly shot to Michael Smith. Ja'Mirra was right. He had hoped to use Michael as his conduit to reshape that abomination they called Earth but now that he was gone he would need someone who could wield the Fabricant.

"True. But I simply don't think I can trust you Ja'Mirra."

"No? Then trust this. Unbind my hands."

Allcraft thought for a moment, his dark eyes contemplating her request. He nodded in the direction of a hovering Bargoul and the creature sputtered over to Ja'Mirra and removed her bindings. From the folds of her gown Ja'Mirra produced the book Krys had found at Castle Blanchfield, the gold and spidery writing on the binding shimmering in the candlelight, and threw it towards Allcraft.

"Is that not what you are looking for? There is a problem, however. It is empty. Lillian did something to it, of that I am sure. I was able to recover some but she has . . . hidden the rest somehow. She must have used a Culling Stone but without the stone . . . there is nothing we can do.

Allcraft reached out, eyes wide, and opened the book. The first few pages were blank but then Allcraft located some calligraphic writing.

. . . and through this divine wisdom the world shall know peace. Yet peace cannot come without struggle, peace cannot come without war. The world shall know these as well. And so it shall be written and spoken that the world shall be cast in two, birthed anew from the minds and souls of the Seraphim. It shall start small, a blessed tear, a sacred breech and through this passage a new world shall be forged. The Seraphim shall sing of it eternal.

Allcraft flipped further into the book, scanning for more writing, for more knowledge. He could feel the power of this text even now, trembling under his finger tips. He continued reading.

Of the First Breach

And so it was that we, the Seraphim, embarked on our great undertaking to provide for our progeny a new world; different from our own yet full of life and wonder. And so we make our first tear, the first opening into this new world. The sacred place shall be a reflection of our ultimate goal, a place reflecting back on itself, a natural formation of Serafina seemingly created to cradle this first breach. From here we shall pass into eternal twilight, sacrificing our sentient lives so that our progeny may have something much, much greater.

"Well I must say Ja'Mirra; this certainly seems like the real thing." Allcraft read the few lines over and over again. He could almost feel the power pulsating from the words. "Where did you get this?"

"At Castle Blanchfield in a secret chamber of Lillian VanVargott."

"Lillian VanVargott?" said Allcraft. "And what of the rest? What has that Fabricantress witch," he paused, looking at Ja'Mirra, "no offense; done with the rest of the words?"

"I also have an idea about that," said Ja'Mirra.

Allcraft smiled, the torchlight making his face look dark and twisted.

"Then Ja'Mirra, it seems we are together again. I will try not to kill you this time, but alas, I cannot make any promises."

Chapter 12

▼

The Book

Their first steps into the now abandoned and empty Castle Blanchfield felt like a dusty memory, a sad and somber evocation of a time when the world was different. If Mya had known then what would happen to her home, her parents, her friends, perhaps she would have run away. Perhaps not. The air, now long stale and still, hung around them like drapes. The darkness was thick and everywhere and nocturnal creatures now called this place home instead of the loyal subjects of a once mighty king. They made their way first through the dining hall, illuminating the space with Fabricated light. Michael gazed into the now vacant and destroyed dining room and his mind instantly jumped back to his first visit to this place. He was just a boy then, scared and trying to make sense of what was happening. He clearly remembered crawling through the wine cellar and listening to two men discuss which wine the king of this castle would prefer for supper. He looked now at the long rows of wooden tables, some overturned, others broken in half, and found it hard to believe this room had ever been alive. Goblets and silverware lay scattered on the floor; the fleeing subjects not even bothering to salvage the metal. A slight whiff of rotten food lingered about the place and their footfalls called back to them as they walked through the large hall.

"Mya I'm so sorry for this . . . your home," said Michael as he crept through the darkened hallways with Mya.

"I know Michael. It's not your fault. Besides, this place stopped being my real home a long time ago. Bartlebug saw to that," replied Mya. Michael nodded in agreement and the pair continued on.

"It's just around here," said Mya, leading her brother beyond the dining hall and through a massive archway. "This was where my parents used to dine and through there is our mother's chamber," said Mya, pointing toward another large door across the dark room.

"Is that where the book is?"

"Yes, but below the floor in a secret chamber she kept." Michael nodded.

Shadows danced about them as they walked with their small balls of Fabricated light hovered just over their shoulders. The light, although constant, created an eerie cascade upon the dark walls and both Michael and Mya felt themselves on edge, as if something from the shadows was going to spring on them at any moment. Making their way through the door into Lillian's private chamber Michael saw the devastation in his mother's room, just the same as the rest of the castle. Destroyed furniture and abandoned accoutrements of a wealthy and prosperous family greeted them as they entered the chamber.

"While you were gone mother sent me here to retrieve the book. That Krys woman got here first. I suppose she took it but . . . that wasn't it was it?"

Michael said nothing.

"Do you remember her? Krys, the woman from the Cerulean School?"

"Yes," said Michael, moving his hand over the torn fabric of the bed sheets.

"Here," said Mya, "follow me and watch your step."

Mya led him to the far corner of the room and there, just as she had left it, was the downward leading staircase built right into the floor.

"Down there," said Mya. "There isn't much left . . . Krys burned most of it. I managed to save the books though."

Michael smiled. "I knew you would," he said.

Michael began his decent. The air became cooler with each step he took and as he went down he noticed a distinct scent of mold and decay; like an old library book. When he reached the bottom a room spread out before him, not much bigger than a study. The familiarity of the place struck him at once, even in the aftermath of Krys' fire. A rocking chair, a small oval shaped carpet, a bookcase; all of these things were found in Serafina but Michael instantly recognized them as Earthly. He felt a brief wash of homesickness, a longing for the world he grew up in. He had not felt that way in a long time. Even though the flames had claimed most of the objects in the room, what remained was unmistakably Earthly.

"This is amazing Mya. She wanted to bring some piece of Earth here. I wonder if she had something like this in our house, a memory of her life here . . ." Michael imaged a room in their basement, hidden away, filled with pictures of King Charles and Mya, books from this world, perhaps a strange musical instrument of some kind.

"Is this the one?" said Mya, selecting a book from the shelf and handing it to Michael. It was easy for Mya to locate the book Michael was talking about and she could not believe she had missed it before. The tome looked untouched and perfect, as if the flames of Krys' fire had simply skipped over it.

"Yes, this is the exact one I remember from when I was a kid." Examining the cover, Michael saw exactly what he remembered; a surly pirate standing on a beach, staring at something in the distance, his red bandana and indigo vest flickering from the sea breeze. A massive blue sky with a few pillow-white clouds floated above him as his mates attempted to make it to shore in a small row boat behind him. The title, *Treasure Island*, spilled across the top in big, red letters.

"*Treasure Island*," said Mya. "Sounds exciting."

"It really is," said Michael. Slowly, he opened the cover. He was certain this was the moment; all the pieces fit. What better place to hide something so important? So vital? A place only Michael would ever think to look. He opened the book somewhere near the center.

"Mya," said Michael, flipping through the pages. Mya peered closer, the light from her shoulder illuminating the path of her gaze.

"Michael . . . it's blank. It's all blank. What does it mean?"

Michael could not answer. How could this be?

"I don't know." Michael slammed the book, his heart a mix of anger and desperation. "What was she thinking? What is her damn plan and why all these secrets!"

"Michael . . . its okay, I'm sure she knows what she is doing."

Michael thought for a moment. He thought about the Departure ceremony and what his mother told him as she lay dying.

"What if this is the right book?" he said, his eyes wide and staring at Mya. "What if our mother made it blank to hide it from Allcraft? You said Krys took the book mom sent you here to get?"

Mya nodded, her mind keeping pace with Michael's and thinking the same thing.

"So Krys took the decoy," said Mya, "and now we have the real thing? Then why is it blank?"

"That is a very good question Mya. If mom somehow . . . transferred the words from the original book into this one then she must have moved them again, I guess to keep them double safe or something. How could someone do something like that Mya?"

Mya thought for a moment.

"A Culling Stone."

"A Culling Stone? What's that?" asked Michael.

"A very rare and very sacred object, I have never seen one, only read about them. They are said to amplify the power of the Fabricant. Many believe they are only a myth but with a Culling Stone . . ."

"Mom could have hidden the words. But where?"

Mya shrugged. "At least Allcraft doesn't have it. That's something."

In the darkness of his mother's secret room Michael felt his heart sink.

CHAPTER 13

BACK TO THE BATHROOM

"Do you remember this place Michael?" He had not been paying much attention to the path Mya took from the castle. As they walked, Michael flipped through the blank pages of what had once been *Treasure Island,* (now it was just a blank green cover, the pirate dust jacket left in Lillian's secret room) convinced something would speak to him, pop out at him; something. He just felt this was right; but why was the book blank?

"Huh?" He replied, looking up from the book. The sun was just setting beyond the horizon and the air felt still, almost peaceful. Michael had trouble remembering the last time he felt the warm breeze on his back, that feeling of everything being at ease.

"Look there," said Mya, pointing a few yards ahead of them. Michael recognized the landmark instantly.

"This was where we first met," he said, walking toward the old tree stump. Looking back Michael could see Castle Blanchfield in the distance. When he first arrived in Serafina the castle had been under some kind of enchantment and Michael had been unable to see it. Now, even at this distance, the castle looked dark.

"Do you remember all those roses? I used to love them so much . . ." Without even speaking the Word, Mya Fabricated a rose. It just popped up from the ground, deep red and very out of place jutting from the hard and cracking ground.

"I do Mya. It was like the color was . . . too much for my eyes."

"I miss it Michael," she said. Her eyes were heavy and dark, her long blonde hair falling about her shoulders in an unkempt mess. "I miss the sunsets, the lazy afternoons. I miss it."

"So do I Mya." He moved toward her and took her hand. "Those days will come again. I promise." He kissed her cheek, brotherly and tender, a gesture of love and understanding.

"Thank you Michael," she said.

"Close your eyes," Michael said. She did. Michael, holding his sister's hand, could feel that familiar Magicant feeling welling inside him. It happened without really thinking about it, he shifted as he had that very first time in this very field, he could feel the distant brush of Twilight as his body sped past it and then they were on Earth.

"Open your eyes Mya," said Michael.

"I have been here before you know. I shifted here once. I guess we share that too," said Mya. Michael nodded. Mya remembered the strange room with the doors and odd smell of the place, the massive twin glass on the wall and the overwhelming feeling of being trapped.

"This is where it first happened, right there in that stall," he said, pointing to the dark green toilet stall. Above, one lonesome light flickered on and off. Neither Michael nor Mya noticed how quiet it was in the school.

"I was thinking about Mom." Mya could see a twinge of deep sadness dance across her brother's face even in this dim light at the mention of their mother. "And then it just happened and there you were, sitting in that rose field."

"I'm glad. I'm glad I was able to meet you," she said, smiling. "I just hope . . . what was that?"

A noise and a flash of movement from the shadows caught Mya's attention.

"I'm not sure," said Michael, slipping the blank book into his waist band. "Come on."

Together they slowly crept across the tile floor of the bathroom and out into the school corridor. The bathroom door swung open with a soft creak. Only a few sparse lights still worked in the hallway and the long corridor was covered in shadow, electric fireflies dancing above them.

"Why is it so dark?" asked Mya.

"I'm not sure. Usually the school is open around this . . ." the noise again, from further down the hall, caused Michael to stop mid sentence and listen, intently. He heard it once more, a shuffle and perhaps a sound, a moan or laugh?

"Light," said Michael. Nothing happened. He allowed himself a small laugh. "Right. Earth."

Slowly they made their way down the hall, holding their breath, waiting for whatever was responsible for the noise to jump at them at any second. As they neared the end of the hallway a sharp right turn greeted them. Michael had walked this hallway everyday to Math class and he knew what to expect around the corner. What he saw instead destroyed him.

"By the Seraphim . . ." gasped Mya. Michael, realizing what stood before him, dropped to his knees. The knowledge hit him hard and fast, a sick realization; this was the culmination of his actions over the past few years with Lucas Allcraft. This sight, this horrible nightmare, was his doing.

"Mya . . . I . . ."

Instead of the hallway where Michael's Math classroom should have been was, simply, nothing. A few feet down the hallway the building, the ground, the sky . . . just stopped. In their place a gaping, black void. In a few places pink and red emanations jettisoned this way and that, seeping from the hole in the world. Physics and gravity had no reign in the void and Michael noticed odd pieces of school equipment falling at wrong angles, moving up and sideways, desks and chairs. The sound disturbed him the most; a strange hissing, like air being let out of a tire. The purple and pink swirl looked like outer space but with no stars. Mya and Michael both felt tears swell in their eyes.

"I did this . . . I destroyed my own world."

The void rose upward as far as Michael could see, blocking out the setting sun and the orange sky. It pulsated, heartbeat-like, and in a few places red and blue puffs of ethereal smoke rose from the inky Twilight beyond the tear.

"It's like the world is . . ."

"Gone," said the voice. Michael and Mya jumped. Rising to his feet, Michael spun around to locate the source of the voice.

"The world is gone now . . . everything is gone now . . ."

From a room in the corner emerged a large figure; broad shoulders, buzz hair cut and massive forearms. The owner of the voice wore a football jacket with the letter L on the front; Levi High School. As soon as the figure moved into the flickering light from one of the overhanging fluorescents Michael recognized him; although he was much older and bigger.

"Jacob?"

"My whole family is gone now . . ."

Mya noticed the clothes Jacob wore were torn and tattered, smudged with dirt. He must have been wearing them for days.

"Jacob . . . do you remember me? Michael Smith?"

Jacob sat down, legs crossed, right in front of them.

"You see that thing? They're everywhere. All over town. New ones pop up every day . . . and not just here. Everywhere . . ."

"Everywhere?" said Michael, turning back to the void.

"I came home and there it was . . . a huge black hole where my house used to be . . . I was out with my friends . . ."

"Jacob . . ." said Michael.

"I tried to find them . . . I looked all over but I didn't want to get too close . . . I threw a baseball into that thing and it vanished. Do you have any food?" Jacob was in shock, his eyes blurry and unfocused.

"I'm sorry . . ."

"It's okay. I have a secret stash . . ." Suddenly he looked at them hard, his eyes instantly turning angry. "Are you here to steal my food?" His voice raised and he jumped up.

"No, not at all . . . Jacob . . ."

"No! I won't let you know!"

Before Michael could react Jacob grabbed him and slammed him against the wall, hard. His head smashed against the concrete and he felt a headache instantly form in his brain.

"Michael!" shouted Mya. "Let him go!" Mya looked for something to hit Jacob with, to get him off of Michael, but there was nothing around them.

"I need my food! I won't be able to survive without it! I . . . need my . . . food!" Jacob screamed and pulled Michael away from the wall, throwing him toward the void. Michael staggered backward and fell to his back, dangerously close to the massive black hole in the world. He could feel the power of it make all his hair stand on end.

"Mya! Run!" shouted Michael, waving his hand for her to come toward him. She understood at once, shared a quick glance with Jacob, and they both charged forward at Michael. She had to get there first. Reaching out his hand, Michael extended it as far as he could and watched Mya sprint toward him. He would have to time it perfectly.

"NOOO!" shouted Jacob Niles as he ran, crazed, toward Michael.

"Now!" shouted Mya, reaching Michael's outstretched hand moments before Jacob crashed into them both. Michael was ready and the instant Mya touched him he shifted, vanished and Jacob was gone, along with the hallway and the half-vanished school where Michael had once eaten grilled cheese sandwiches.

Opening his eyes, he glanced around to see they were back in Serafina, not far from the stump. The sun had set fully now and the moon rose in the distance, a white ball of light casting them in half-light.

"Are you alright Mya?"

"Yes, I think so."

Michael sat on the ground, head between his legs. Mya found a spot next to him and, placing her arm around his shoulders, attempted to offer him some small comfort.

"It's not your fault. It is Allcraft's fault. And there has to be a way to set things right."

"My home . . . my world . . . it's destroyed."

There was nothing else Mya could say. Allcraft had used Michael, for nearly two years, to tear breaches into the fabric of the worlds; dark voids made of nothing, the Fabrication that was Earth ceasing to be. Eventually the Singing will end and Earth will be gone for good and Mya knew the only way to save Earth was to stop Allcraft . . . if that would even be enough. Was the damage too great already?

"Michael come on, we have to get back. Maybe Quixitix knows something about this book. Michael nodded and reluctantly stood. He concentrated for a moment on Quixitix' home in Aside and a portal opened, wavering and shimmering in the darkness.

"There is always hope Michael, even in the darkest night. You just have to look for the light," said Mya, as they stepped into the portal and left the barren field behind.

Excerpt from the final issue of *The New York Times*.

Front page only.

One story.

World Governments Prepare Quarantine, New York Times Closes Doors.

Terri Wilson, Editor in Chief

In reaction to the recent devastating and unexplained global events, world governments have begun setting up and enforcing quarantine zones in major cities. The entire world waits to see what will happen and what exactly is going on as cities are swallowed up into enormous dark voids.

New York City has suffered the same fate as many other major, world cities. Central park is gone, replaced by a massive black hole. Thousands are dead and the White House has ordered an evacuation of New York City. New York is not alone. Los Angeles, Philadelphia and many other populated areas across the U.S. have already begun evacuations. Where no anomalies have been reported the government has begun establishing temporary housing and shelter for the displaced citizens although statements from Washington encourage people to bring tents, campers and other self-sufficient means of survival as they flee their homes.

The offices of the New York Times no longer stand. One week ago a void appeared here and devastated our offices and print facilities. Torn in half and gone in an instant, we can no longer sustain and this will be our final print publication. We can only *pray and hope for our future and attempt to weather this storm as best we can as one nation, joined together by a common instinct to survive and hope that tomorrow the sun will still rise and Earth's people will still have a world to call home. For now, stay calm, find a safe place and pray for a better tomorrow.*

CHAPTER 14

▼

CARRIED AWAY

Since their return from the White Loam, Quixitix found himself spending a great deal of time with Lucious and Lavinia. His concern for them, of course, went far beyond curiosity and science, but their fate enthralled him like few things did. The twins were fascinating to him, living relics of another world. He felt the same intrigue and interest he felt when he first met Michael all those years ago and the boy recognized the soda can sitting atop a pedestal in the workshop; another relic from a world Quixitix had only glimpsed. That metallic can seemed a distant and pale memory compared to the things Quixitix had seen since; towering sky scrapers, fast moving cars, and even airplanes. The machinations of Earth, many of which Quixitix brought back to Serafina in order to study and track the growing number of tears in the fabric of the worlds, were marvels all their own.

"That is actually quite good Lavinia," said Quixitix, turning the object over in his hands. "I am impressed by this seam work here. Did you use the wielder?"

"Yes," said Lavinia, nodding. She often found herself working with Quixitix in his shop. She identified with the tinkering and the feel of metal things; cold, unfeeling. It reminded her of the way she felt deep inside; empty and cold. That feeling was fading a little now though, after whatever Michael did to them at that place.

"And what about this," said Quixitix. He held a small sphere made of shiny metal. Twisting the small, metal ball and popping off the top, Quixitix heard an audible pop and looked in the sphere. Inside, wires of several different colors wound through the guts of the small object. "You wired it all," he said mostly to himself.

"Yes. Press the button on the side."

Quixitix twisted the top half of the ball back into place and did as Lavinia had instructed. When he depressed the button, the device hummed for a moment and then began playing a melody, something slow and peaceful.

"A music box?" said Quixitix.

"Yes. But I made it play three different songs. You see that plate there? Where your thumb is? That will sense how hot your hands are. The hotter your hands, the more soothing the music. If your hand is cool, one of the faster songs will play."

"Ingenious Lavinia," he said, handing the orb back to her.

"I made it for Michael," she said, taking the orb from Quixitix. He smiled down at her and in that moment Lavinia's mind shuffled back to her first encounter with Michael Smith in the antique shop. She could remember feeling something, even then, although now feelings were difficult to discern and even more difficult to understand. Without her Ember, her soul, she could not really, truly feel anything. Michael had at least given her something, a temporary salve, to help her feel normal, but all she really wanted was to feel more than she could. She knew Michael was special.

"He will love it," said Quixitix. "I'm certain he could use some comfort, especially now."

Lavinia nodded.

"Where is Lucious?"

"I think he is in our room. Reading maybe."

"Okay. I will be back soon," said Quixitix. "I am going into town for some food for supper."

"Alright," said Lavinia, turning away from Quixitix and placing the orb on the wooden table. As she did so both Lavinia and Quixitix heard a loud thud on the roof of the workshop. The impact was slight but it was enough to cause the spherical music box to begin rolling, slowly, toward the edge of the workbench.

"What was that?" asked Lavinia.

"I don't know. Stay here," said Quixitix. From the wall Quixitix took down his Caliber and loaded a fresh bolt into the device. He slung the quiver of Caliber bolts onto his back. Lavinia listened to the audible click the weapon made when it was being loaded but did not notice her music box fall from the work table and roll across the floor a few feet away.

"I'm going to check on Lucious," she said. Quixitix nodded and walked toward the front door. Everything was silent in the workshop except for the sound of Quixitix' light footsteps. He opened the front door slowly, peering out as he did so. The day was warm and in the distance he could see Aside, smoke rising from one of the chimneys in town. Glancing to the left and the right he saw nothing so Quixitix ventured further outside. He walked a few paces away from the workshop and again scanned the surrounding area; nothing. Then he turned back and glanced up.

There, on the roof, was the source of the sound he and Lavinia had heard moments before. The sight of it made Quixitix reel for a moment. Laying on the roof, upside down and brutalized, was the body of a Bargoul. Fluids dripped from its wounds and were making their way down the slanted roof surface. One of the creature's wings was completely missing and Quixitix could see the creature had suffered a great deal before meeting its end. He did not recognize the Bargoul but he had a feeling it was not one of Allcraft's. He inched closer, staring up at the body, and in that moment of distraction the trap was sprung.

From all sides of the building, Bargouls flooded at Quixitix, wings buzzing in a thunderous cacophony. The noise was enough to distract and stun Quixtix who had only moments to react.

"Monsters!" shouted Quixitix, firing the Caliber as fast as he could. Still a dangerous marksman, Quixitix managed to hit one or two, but there were simply too many of them.

"We need the boy!" shouted one of the Bargouls. "Where is Smith!"

"You'll never have him!" shouted Quixitix, jumping to the ground and narrowly avoiding the stinger of one particularly massive Bargoul.

"Obviously he isn't here now to protect *you*!" shouted another one, coming at Quixitix. He reloaded the Caliber, his nimble hands moving very quickly to the quiver, and fired the bolt, striking the Bargoul directly in the body. Greyish fluid sprayed from the wound and the Bargoul hit the ground, dust pluming upward from the impact of his body.

Quixitix made for the workshop door but several Bargouls were blocking it. He only had a few bolts left; not nearly enough to kill them all.

"Nowhere to run," said the largest of the Bargouls. He landed on the ground and inched his way toward Quixitix. "Master Allcraft will have his way old human."

"Never. Michael will stop you. And Mya. You will never win."

"We already have."

Just then the workshop door burst open sending the Bargouls standing in front of it to the ground in a heap. From the opening emerged Dunny, squeezing his way through the frame, barely making it.

"Brother!" he shouted, swatting at the Bargouls closest to him with his massive hands. He connected with two of them and sent them flying in different directions. Several others attempted to pierce him with their stingers and Dunny managed to avoid a few but the swarm was too much and some of them found their mark, drawing fresh blood from Dunny's body.

He screamed, not from pain but from rage; not caring about the wounds or the blood, only wanting to protect his brother from the attack. He rushed forward, charging into a cluster of the attacking Bargouls until he stood in front of Quixitix, his massive body protecting the older man.

"Now have at you creatures!" shouted Dunny, his anger palpable.

"Fools. You have played your parts perfectly," said the largest Bargoul, hovering in front of them. He floated higher while Dunny and Quixitix watched. Suddenly a portion of the workshop roof exploded into splinters and dust. From the newly formed hole Dunny and Quixtix watched as several Bargouls hoisted a large bed sheet into the air. The sheet seemed to be writhing and moving and the weight of it seemed great.

"No, no!" shouted Quixitix. He was a good shot, but he could not risk hitting what he now realized was scrambling in that blanket. "No, you can't have them again!"

"We already have them!" said the leader, floating up to join the Bargouls carrying the blanket. Quixitix fired a shot at him but missed, only slightly.

"No, Dunny! We have to save them!" he shouted, running after the blanket floating through the sky. Quixitix and Dunny ran after them on foot, kicking up dust as they moved across the hardpan, but the Bargouls moved too fast and soon they were out of reach entirely. The attack was over. Lucious and Lavinia were gone.

"Dunny . . ." Quixitix dropped to the ground, his brother putting his large arm around his back.

"Michael will save them," said Dunny. "'e will."

"I don't know this time Dunny. I failed them . . ."

As he watched the Bargouls disappear, Quixitix saw something fall from the blanket, just catching a ray of light as it fell, sending it glinting toward Quixitix. Standing, he ran toward the object and found it nestled in the grass. It was the orb Lavinia made for Michael. Quixitix picked it up and heard the device whirr to life. It began playing a very soft, soothing melody, the melancholy notes floating up toward Lucious and Lavinia as they were carried away again to the waiting hands of Lucas Allcraft.

CHAPTER 15

▼

TWILIGHT CREATURES

He sat king-like, his face a smirk, as he twirled a strand of his long hair in the dark room. In his other hand floated two small, burning ghosts of light. One blue, one red. As they hovered in his open hand they cast light at strange angles on his grim face. So pure, these two Embers. So innocent, so young. Lucas examined them, stared into them as he so often did, as if staring at a vast ocean; beautiful and mysterious at the same time.

"Those belong to us," said a meek voice from the other side of the room.

"I know. But I had to take them so I could be whole again. You are, after all, my blood. Did you know that?"

Lucious said nothing from the shadows. He wanted nothing to do with the monster before him.

"You're a monster," said the other voice, as if reading her brother's mind.

"A monster? Oh no, no child." Allcraft stood and the Embers floated toward his chest, disappearing through the dark cloth of his half unbuttoned shirt. "I am no monster. I only want what I deserve, what I have worked for my entire life. I want the tyranny of the Fabricantresses to vanish forever and I want to forge a new world, free of their shackles."

Lavinia, in stark indignation of her captor's words, rattled the metal bindings around her wrists. "You mean shackles like these?" she said.

"A necessary precaution. I need you now that Michael Smith is gone. I suppose I knew he would eventually abandon me . . . lasted longer than I thought, actually. It doesn't matter now. He played his part and the other world is crumbling; the Song is ending and it is time for a new one to be sung."

Lavinia gazed around the cold room as Allcraft spoke, looking for a way out. The only exit she could see was a small window on the far wall. Through the window she could see only blue sky and a few wispy, white clouds. She figured they were in a tower of some kind; too high to jump.

"Where are we?" she demanded. Lucious remained silent beside her.

"My home," replied Allcraft, "for the time being at least." He continued pacing around the room, his yellowed teeth peeking out from behind his sinister smile. "Care to have a look?"

Allcraft motioned for Lavinia to approach the window but she sat motionless, glaring at him. "Brave girl," he said. "Bartlebug!"

From behind her Lavinia heard a door open and then close abruptly. Seconds later the familiar sound of buzzing Bargoul wings floated to her ears as Bartlebug hovered past her.

"Bring her here," commanded Allcraft. Bartlebug complied and roused Lavinia to her feet forcefully. She struggled a bit but soon realized there was no point. Hands bound, she walked toward the window with Bartlebug at her back.

"What do you see there?" said Allcraft, cocking his head toward the window. Bartlebug shoved Lavinia closer and she peered out from the tower window.

She had guessed correctly; they were high up, very high up. At first glance she felt a sense of vertigo; the ground reeling away from her and everything getting smaller. The feeling soon passed and her eyes took in the sight. A beautiful landscape spread out before her; trees, rolling green hills and a tiny river cutting through the countryside. In the distance; snow capped mountains.

"Lovely, isn't it?" said Allcraft. Lavinia said nothing but he was right; it was beautiful. "Look there," said Allcraft, pointing toward a small glade in the middle of the trees. At first Lavinia could see nothing in the clearing but then her eyes adjusted and she wasn't sure what they saw.

"What is it?" she said.

"Watch closely," said Allcraft. He closed his eyes, slowly, and took a deep breath. His brow furrowed and Bartlebug used his small, sooty hand to turn her head away from Allcraft and back toward the clearing. Seconds passed and soon Lavinia began to see a glimmer begin to move and shift, waver in the sunlight. She watched as it grew bigger and became more agitated. After a moment the color of the glimmer began to change as well, going from translucent to inky purple, velvet and blue. The colors seemed to swim in and out of each other, mixing and forming together, pulling apart and creating something incredible.

"What you are looking at girl," said Allcraft, "is the pure essence of Twilight. The ether from which your kind draw their power and from which the Magicans draw theirs. This is The Twinning, raw and unbridled, spilling into this world from Twilight."

Lavinia could not help but stare at the sight. It looked like water pouring out of thin air in the small clearing, only colored with fantastic hues.

"Our work is complete, as you can see. The Song of the Seraphim can no longer contain The Twinning, nor can it control its power. But I can." Allcraft closed his eyes again, concentrating, his fists clenched as if gripping something tightly. Lavinia, eyes fixed on the clearing, watched intently. As she realized what was happening her feelings of awe and beauty quickly changed to horror and fear.

From the swirling ether came a creature; massive and made of the same misty gauze as the stuff flowing from the clearing. Even from this height Lavinia could make out arms and legs, a tail with protruding spikes thrashing this way and that, horns, claws . . . a nightmare creature. The beast opened its mouth and bellowed a scream so loud it shook the walls of the tower they currently inhabited. Then it stopped and simply gazed up at the tower, waiting for orders.

"I control Twilight now. I command it. Nightmares, dreams, power, wisdom . . . it all comes from the Twinning and thanks to Michael Smith I have inherited the right to harness that power." From beneath his shirt Allcraft pulled a pendant attached to a chain hanging from his neck. At the end of the pendant a glowing red ruby, perfectly cut, hung like a drop of blood.

"Every time he destroyed one, its power entered this one. Every time I convinced him to silent a Seraphim, their song flitted into this stone. Now there are more gone than remain and their power exists here, with me. But it is still not enough." Allcraft placed the stone back into the safety of his shirt. "I still need a Fabricantress. So I have a gift for you."

Allcraft extended his arm and opened his hand, palm up. A second passed and then Lavinia's Ember appeared above his open palm. He made a small gesture and the glowing flame moved from Allcraft's hand toward Lavinia's chest.

"You may have this back. I will need your power come the end. You are, after all, my own flesh and blood."

The floating fire entered Lavinia's chest and she instantly felt her body shiver and the heat of her soul flowed through her again. The change was instantaneous; her eyes burst with life, her heart raced and she could feel a will inside her that she had not felt in a very long time.

"I will never help you," she said, renewed with great courage and determination.

"Oh, but you will girl," said Allcraft. Below, the beast bellowed again and Lavinia glanced out the window once more, watching as more creatures began to spew from the ether in the clearing, each one a different shape and size but all culled from dark and desperate nightmares. A scream from across the room brought her attention back to Allcraft. She spun and saw three Bargouls hovering about her brother, stingers at the ready, one of them so close it was pressing into Lucious' neck.

Lavinia turned to Allcraft. "Do not hurt him," she commanded.

"As you wish m'lady, so long as you do what I want. Take him!" shouted Allcraft. The Bargouls picked Lucious up from the spot where he sat and carried the boy out of the room. Lavinia could hear his screams as he was dragged down the hall and away from her. She wanted only to chase after him, to destroy those Bargouls and save him. But she knew she could not do that.

"I'll do what you want," she said.

"Of course you will," said Allcraft, turning back to the window and looking down upon his creatures, his army now poised to raze this world on his quest to create a new one.

CHAPTER 16

▼

IT BEGINS

Michael's eyes opened slowly, his sleep interrupted by the slants of warm sunlight sneaking through the shuttered windows of his room. The bed was warm and comfortable; his head resting peacefully on a down pillow, the feathers courtesy of one of Serafina's most sought after creatures; a large bird called a Diatryma. His mind rose easily to the surface of consciousness and he soon began to take in other stimuli; the far off sound of birds chirping somewhere, the smell of coffee brewing (here it was called kafee) and the familiar creaking and moaning of the boards forming the upstairs of Quixitix' home. A knock at the door woke him fully.

"Michael?" said his sister, her voice soft, from the behind the door. "Are you up yet?"

"Yea," said Michael, rolling over in the bed and landing his feet on the small carpet below. From the chair standing next to his bed he grabbed his shirt and tossed it over his head, pulling his long hair from the collar.

"Quixitix and Dunny are waiting. They made breakfast," said Mya, entering the room. As she did she noticed Michael pulling the hair from his collar and his shirt was not quite covering him fully. In the seconds before he pulled down the shirt Mya noticed several scars and wounds on Michael's back.

"Michael . . ." she said. He knew she had seen the scars.

"It's okay. Sometimes the chambers were guarded . . ." He did not elaborate.

"Some kind of shadow creature?" said Mya, walking over to him. He nodded.

"I saw one once. A few months back, in the Yestersand. I was looking for you."

"I remember the Yestersand. We went there to find a chamber. The creature was ancient, all shadow. I don't know where they come from but we fought it off. I guess it wasn't dead. Did it attack you?" he said, turning and gazing into her eyes.

"No. It just tried to scare me, gave me a warning. I was too late anyway, you were gone."

"I know. I'm sorry Mya," he said, taking her hand in his. "For everything."

She smiled and patted the top of his hand. "It's okay."

From below, a loud voice beckoned them.

"It's ready you two. Get it while it's 'ot!"

Dunny's spirits had much improved the past few weeks, ever since Michael came back.

"Let's go," he said. Together they walked downstairs to find Quixitix and Dunny at the table. Plates and goblets were scattered on the large, wooden surface and Quixitix stood near the stove in the corner intently watching a pan. The sound of something sizzling on the hot surface caused Michael's stomach to rumble.

"Good morning everyone," he said.

"Mornin' Michael," replied Dunny. His voice troubled Michael; once so jubilant and full of life, now it sounded hollow and empty, like a mask.

"Any news about the twins?" Michael had been thinking about them all night, thinking about ways to get them back, where Allcraft might be and worrying if they were okay. Quixitix' guilt was matched only by Michael and Mya's; had they not been back in Blanchfield when the Bargouls attacked, the twins might still be here. Quixitix spoke up.

"Some contacts in town say they saw some Bargouls to the South, a rather large band of them by the man's description, headed toward Everfell Forest. Not much there though," said Quixitix, flipping the contents of the pan, "can't imagine why Allcraft would be in Everfell."

"Alright," said Michael. "Any other ideas where he might be?" No one spoke. Mya sat down at the table and placed a book in front of her. Michael had not even noticed her carrying it.

"Is that the book?" he said. She nodded.

"Any ideas about that?" said Michael. He watched as Mya flipped through the blank pages; page after page of nothingness. She examined the cover, just a simple shade of blue, no writing, no title.

"None," she said. "Do you think this is the book mother wanted us to find?"

"Absolutely," said Michael. "I'm sure of it. We just have to figure out what it means."

Dunny sat down loudly opposite Michael and Mya.

"That the Song of the Seraphim then? Can't believe it 'elly exists," said Dunny. "They say that tome there is responsible for the creation of the world. The Seraphim used it to map out the place, jot it all down, catalogue it. Why's it blank then?"

Michael and Mya said nothing. From the corner Quixitix began placing the sweet sausages and eggs on plates for the quartet. They sat together quietly, enjoying the meal as best they could with such heavy minds. Moments such as these were seldom and each of the four companions felt it essential to enjoy them when they came. As they finished the meal the door of the kitchen crashed open loudly and through the portal burst Sven, a farmer from Aside. He was sweating and clearly agitated having run all the way from town to Quixitix' domicile. His face, stark and frightened, told Michael and Mya everything before he even began talking.

"The town . . . it's under siege. Please, hurry, they're destroying everything! Creatures, massive . . . made of shadows . . ." Sven was terrified and talking very fast.

"Sven, slow down. What happened?" said Quixitix.

"They came from the canyon, started pouring out of it this morning. They're burning the town, killing . . . please hurry!"

"Let's go Mya," said Michael, jumping up from the table. Mya rose as well and grabbed her satchel from a small hook on the wall, slung it around her body, placed the book inside, and was ready to go.

"Quixitix, Dunny, stay here," said Michael. They agreed.

"Michael, here," said Quixitix as Michael made his way toward the door. The old professor tossed something in Michael's direction, a small, metal ball. "Lavinia wanted you to have that," he said. Michael looked down at the sphere, spun it around in his hand feeling the smooth metal.

"Thank you," said Michael. Quixitix nodded.

"Sven, lead the way," said Michael, putting the sphere in his pocket.

Michael and Mya followed Sven out of Quixitix' home and did not think to glance back at the two brothers sitting at the kitchen table. If they had, it would have been the last time they would have ever seen them alive.

▼

THE RAZING OF ASIDE

"Move!" shouted Mr. Mayweather, grabbing his wife and pushing her and his children out of their home. The foundation shook and the children screamed as a throaty, deep growl surrounded them. From the kitchen, pots and dishes slammed to the floor, shattering into pieces. The smell of ash and singed hair filled the hallway as the Mayweather's fled to the front door, trying to avoid the sound from the back of the house. From the windows, they could see others running past the house, fleeing down the cobblestone streets, away from whatever manner of creature owned the growl growing louder and more ferocious with each passing second.

"Go!" At last they reached the front door and plowed through it, bursting into the sunlight and down the steps into the street. Glancing back, Mr. Mayweather saw the beast approaching his home; it towered over the house, taller by two leagues. Its skin was made of what looked like smoke and water, purple and yellow in places, moving and undulating like a rapid river. The thing's eyes glowed red and it slashed through the air with massive hands, sharp claws cutting through the trees in the backyard of the Mayweather home.

"Faster!" Madeline and her mother followed Mr. Mayweather, running through the streets behind him. Trevor kept pace with his father and only glanced back once;

it was all he needed. As they ran, they heard the splintering and shattering sound of wood and glass ripping apart; their home was no more.

"Charlie!" shouted Mr. Mayweather, nearly running into another man as they made their way through the cross street and into another part of town.

"By the Seraphim get out! What are these things!" Charlie's eyes were solid and struck with fear. Mr. Mayweather tried to ignore his own dread but it skittered all over his face. "This way!"

Following Charlie, the family ran South down Pigeon Street toward the market district. Smoke and dust billowed from behind buildings and a few structures had caught fire already, the attack too rapid and unexpected. From behind them they heard the screams of townsfolk mixed with the roars of the creatures.

"What are they Charlie?" asked Mr. Mayweather as they ran.

"No idea," replied Charlie, panting. "Word is they came from the Canyon, just poured out of there."

"How many are there?"

"I don't know. Twenty, fifty. Huge. We have no chance against them."

They ran, crashing around overturned food carts and rubble, dodging other people trying to get away. To their left, a building exploded out toward them sending debris raining down around them; one large board fell on Madeline and she cried out, but her mother helped her up and they continued moving.

"Stop!" shouted Mr. Mayweather. They were nearly at the market district and the edge of town; they could see the rolling green hills sprawling into the distance and the dirt road leading to Quixitix' place. As they came to a halt, a creature much like the one responsible for the destruction of the Mayweather's home crept from behind the Inn. This one was pig-like, with floppy ears and a massive snout; not as big as the other one but with the same glowing, red eyes.

"Don't move," said Charlie. They stood as still as they could, trembling as the creature stalked in front of them, praying it would pass them by.

It snorted once and stopped, glancing away from them, toward the hills. Then it turned toward them and its eyes lanced straight through Mr. Mayweather. It howled, long and fierce, then turned its body toward them.

"What do we do?" said Trevor, looking toward his father. Mr. Mayweather had no time to think, no time to consider options. He had to keep his family safe. Going back meant death. Going forward meant facing this creature. He couldn't think.

Suddenly, from the pig-creature's chest, a massive ball of fire exploded and the beast let out a wail so loud the children covered their ears and even Charlie hunched over in pain. Mr. Mayweather watched as the creature swayed back and forth, staggering, gripping the wound in its center, the light from the sky falling through its translucent and wavering skin, droplets of purple ooze pouring from the gap. Another ball of fire burst from the pig's knee sending the giant crashing to the ground; the road shook as the beast's other knee landed hard.

"What's happening to it?" shouted Madeline.

"I don't know!" said Mr. Mayweather.

Finally, a hot-blue fire ball burst through the pig's face, sending gloomy fragments of ether flying in all directions. What was left of the creature toppled to the ground in front of the shocked crowd.

"Look!" shouted Charlie.

From behind the pig a figure, head down and breathing hard, walked toward them. Even at that distance his eyes burst with light, confidence and anger. His long, black hair seemed to hover around his shoulders as he walked down the road, past the motionless and hulking body of the pig creature; he did not even look at it. To his right, a woman. The same look in her eyes; fierce determination mingled with unbridled anger. Mr. Mayweather recognized them immediately.

"Michael! Mya!" he shouted. They waved and approached. Trevor Mayweather watched the duo coming toward him. For a moment he imagined they were both Seraphim, like in the stories his mother used to tell before bed, come to save them all.

"Are you alright?" asked Michael when he got close enough.

"Yes, I think so," replied Mrs. Mayweather. As they spoke, Mya noticed something move behind one of the half-destroyed buildings and she reacted, almost without thought. She no longer needed the Word to assist her; her pure thought was enough. In seconds, the Shield of the Seraphim formed around the ground and as it rose around them in a sphere, a massive ball of inky purple muck rocketed toward them. When it hit the Shield, the projectile exploded into a massive shower of pink and purple fragments, falling all around them and painting the street. The creature who threw the object screamed and jumped from behind the building, clearing it completely, and landing only a few yards from the group. This creature was tall and lanky; it's limbs longer than its body and out of proportion. Its head twitched at odd angles and clicked back and forth, extended and insect-like.

"Get back!" shouted Michael. He shot a sideways glance at Mya and she understood at once, without the need for words. She waved her hand and a series of stone steps appeared in front of Michael; he began leaping upon them as they formed, jumping to the next one before it was even there. After a few steps he leapt into the air and flew up, toward the creature's head, moving faster than Mya had ever seen him move before. The creature was fast too.

With a blinding movement, the insect-creature slashed with its huge arm and connected with Michael's body, sending him crashing into the town clock tower.

"Michael!" shouted Mya. At her voice, the insect-creature looked in her direction. She reacted, quickly, and ran toward the creature's legs. As she ran, she Fabricated an elongated, double sided blade that ran from one end of the street to the other with Mya at its center. Running, she shot the weapon away from her and toward the creature's legs. It connected and the creature screamed with pain as the blades sliced through its ankles. Mya watched the blades go through the thing's legs and then the legs reformed instantly. She stopped and looked at the clock tower. She did not see Michael.

The creature bellowed loudly at Mya and moved to strike at her, reeling back with its arm, prepared to smash her into the ground. It never got the chance.

With blinding speed, Michael shot through the air and, with the flaming fires of the Magicant surrounding his balled fists, slammed his entire body through the creatures arm. The blow was too much for the creature and severed its arm in two, half the murky, purple appendage falling to the street below. The insect-creature screamed, an angry scream, and shot its other arm toward Michael, who dodged it easily.

"Mya! Now!" shouted Michael, hovering above.

Mya concentrated and pictured the object in her mind, pictured where she wanted it and how it would come into existence.

The insect-creature screamed and then grew silent, as if confused. Gripping its chest, the creature staggered and scowled at Mya. Then, from within, the insect-creature exploded as a massive ball of translucent light expanded from inside its chest like an enormous bubble filled with sun. The creature emitted one last, agonized scream, and fell to the ground in a massive pile of ethereal goo.

Michael flew toward the ground and landed, hard, bracing himself with his knee and his hand. He rose, and walked toward Mya.

"You okay?" he said.

"Yes. How many are there?" she said, slightly winded.

"A lot. We can't fight them all. We have to get out of here. Mr. Mayweather?" said Michael, motioning for the family and Charlie to come out from the alley they had been hiding in.

"Let's go. We can't stay here. Aside is gone. I'm sorry." Michael looked back at the town and watched the tendrils of smoke rise from the snaking streets, listening to the sounds of destruction as the homes and shops were destroyed by these horrible creatures.

"I just hope some survived," said Michael. "Come on. We have to go now. Mya, can you take them back to Quixitix' place? I'm going to look for other survivors."

"Michael, it's too dangerous, let me come with you."

"Mya, please. Save them. I'll be fine." He smiled, gripping her shoulders. "Please."

She nodded and rounded up the group, leading them away. "Take this at least," she said. From her belt Mya pulled the book they had found at Castle Blanchfield, void of any writing and containing only blank pages. Michael looked at her as she tossed the tome to him, wondering what good the blank pages would do him. "You never know," she said, walking away with the Mayweathers and Charlie.

She glanced back at Michael, standing there in the street, his long, dark hair falling at jagged angles on his shoulders, the sun rising behind him in orange and red hues. She nodded and he returned the signal, watching them hurry toward the hills.

Michael turned to face Aside.

"Allcraft. This is enough," he said out loud. "This ends now."

In the distance a soft and subtle thunderclap rang out, barely heard, yet a grim harbinger of the looming storm.

CHAPTER 18

▼

IN COUPLET CANYON ONCE MORE

By the time he reached Couplet Canyon, night had fallen and the stars were the only light glinting down upon the dirt and grass. Aside had been ravaged and the town no longer stood; the horizon showed plumes of smoke from the burned and destroyed buildings. Michael had walked through streets covered in fiery ash, examining the torn buildings and the bodies of the dead. This time Allcraft was serious; the end was coming, Michael was certain of it. On his way to the canyon he had fought several Twilight creatures; he was sure now that is where they came from. The way they reacted to the Magicant, the way they boiled over and spewed onto the floor when he killed them; he knew they were culled from the ether of the Twinning and he was certain Allcraft commanded them.

It was quiet now and Michael had a few moments to think about his first visit to Aside; his first encounter with the Mayweathers, his trip to the bakery and his walk down the busy main street. Those feelings felt so far away, like a dream viewed through a glass darkly. He could not quite pinpoint the moment when he no longer felt like a child, like a lost boy wandering through this strange and magical land. He often found himself thinking back across the years between now and then, trying to find that moment. Was it when he made the decision to go with Allcraft? Was it when he questioned everything his mother had told him about the Order and the Fabricantressess? Or was it during those long voyages with Allcraft and Bartlebug, traveling miles and miles to find the next Seraphim chamber, barely talking to each other, lost in his own thoughts? The answer eluded him still and so he continued walking.

The canyon was almost peaceful now as he passed through the bottle neck where once he staged a grand battle between the brave men and women of Aside and the army of Bargouls Allcraft had sent to secure the portal here. As he walked, Michael could feel the Twinning vibrating all around him, causing the hairs on his arms and hands to stand, called to order. The power surged through the canyon, raw and untamed. Things were coming apart.

At last he wandered into the twin canyon itself and stood before a massive tear in the worlds; a gaping hole falling out and into itself, the ether of Twilight and the pure essence of the Twinning pouring through in rivulets and streams. Michael stood transfixed for a few moments, gazing at the unbridled power and majesty of the Twinning in its true form, released from the confines of Twilight. He knew how big his role was in this destruction; he was responsible for it all. Without him, Allcraft would never have gotten this far. He cursed himself, yet again, for being so naive; but that was in the past and the only path forward was to correct the mistakes he made and stop Allcraft for good.

Michael approached the tear, unsure of what he was doing but for some reason moving forward, some unknown force telling him it was okay. The eddy pulsed and vibrated in time with Michael's heart, as if the two were connected, syncopated and in perfect time. In the darkness of the canyon the tear seemed to glow and Michael had trouble judging the actual size of the thing. Soon he was close enough to reach out and touch the undulating tear in the world, his outstretched finger tips dizzy, tingling with anticipation and energy.

Then everything went black.

▼

CHAPTER 19

DUNNY AND QUIXITIX

"No . . ." Mya gasped for breath and felt the salty sting of her own tears as they ran down from her eyes to her lips, pooling there for a moment and then falling to the ground.

"Mya . . ." said Trevor Mayweather, bracing her as she reeled back in disbelief.

The group had fled the monsters attacking Aside with the knowledge that the home of Quixitix Dunmire would be safe and free from attack. They had been wrong.

As they approached the workshop, Madeline was the first to see the smoke rising from the building but she had said nothing, hoping everyone and everything was alright. Then Mr. Mayweather had seen it as well and commanded the group to stop and wait. Mya did not listen and she ran forward, Trevor by her side.

"No," she said again, gazing at the smoldering building; or at least what was left of it. Just next to the rubble was a massive pile of the ooze; a fallen creature. At least they had put up a fight.

"Dunny!" she shouted, running toward the burning building. "Dunny! Quixitix!" No answer, only the sound of burning wood and the smell of fires in the fall. "Dunny!" she shouted again. For a moment she thought she heard something move in the debris; the shifting of wood or the scratch of metal. She looked for the sound, trying to find someone, something; some survivors in the attack.

"Quixitix!" she shouted, running through the rubble. Then she saw him.

The professor's body, wedged under a massive burning board, lay bruised and broken; his clothes in tatters and terrible scorch marks across his face. His hair, singed and much of it gone, stood at odd angles from his head. Mya rushed toward him and threw herself to her knees.

"Hold on," she said. "Help me Trevor!"

Together, Mya and Trevor gripped the burning board, Mya totally oblivious to the pain from the heat and the fire. They lifted and, barely, managed to remove the object from Quixitix' waist.

"Quixitix, Professor!" said Mya, holding his head. "Quixitix!" She placed her ear to his chest and could hear nothing. "No!" She shouted, as the rest of the group arrived at her location and saw the sight before them. "Look for Dunny!" she commanded, and the Mayweathers left without speaking to search the debris for Quixitix' brother.

"Please, answer me!" she shouted again. This time, Quixitix' head moved slightly and his eyes opened to just slits, scanning the face before him.

"Mya . . . I'm sorry. We killed it but . . ." he coughed and Mya watched a small stream of blood trickle from his lips.

"You did great professor," she said. Mya closed her eyes and concentrated, called up the Fabricant, pleading for aid in this most dire circumstance. She placed her hands on Quixitix' chest and called out to the Seraphim, to the Twinning, with all her might. Quixitix smiled.

"I am honored," he said, meagerly. "But this is my time now. I have served my purpose in this fight," he coughed again, harder this time. "Dunny is . . ." he could not finish the statement, he coughed, very hard and more blood trickled from his mouth. "Dunny did not . . ."

"Don't professor," said Mya, holding him, crying. "Just rest."

"Thank you," said Quixitix. "You are powerful Mya. You and your brother can stop all this. You and Michael can make the world right again."

Mya stared at him, unable to say anything. She held him, felt his chest rise up one last time and watched his eyes close softly. A small trace of a smile fell upon his face and then he was gone. Mya laid his body down, ever so softly, away from the burning debris. She wept into her hands, the tears making tracks in the dirt on her face.

"Mya, I'm so sorry," said Madeline, kneeling down next to her and placing her arm around Mya's shoulder.

"We found Dunny," said a voice from the other side of the house. It was Mr. Mayweather and his voice quivered as he spoke. "You should stay there Mya. His body . . . it's bad Mya." She barely heard him. Rage, sadness and pity swelled up in her like a wave, cresting and crashing upon her badly trodden heart. So much pain, so much suffering; when would it end? Who had the power to end it? Did she? Was she the one who could stop it all? How could she? The sound of a falling board brought her attention back to the group. She tried to calm herself, to stop the tears, but couldn't. She needed them to come.

"We . . . will bury . . . them," she said. Everyone nodded. "They were . . . wonderful. They deserve . . . to rest . . . together."

As Michael made his way to Couplet Canyon and the moon rose over Aside, Mya, the Mayweathers and Charlie buried Archibald and Dunmire Quixitix, together, side by side. Few words were said but the words that were spoken were powerful and true. As the night grew to its full dark the company left the hillside upon which they had buried their friends, nearly at the same moment Michael touched the tear in the world and disappeared.

Chapter 20

▼

In The Twinning

He felt warmth and sunlight. At first that was all and that was all he needed to feel. Summer. The lake. Fishing. The bus to school. These memories, crystalline feelings stored in the ether of memory, crashed around him and it felt good. He was surrounded by light and peaceful tranquility. He wanted for nothing and needed nothing.

"Where am I?" His mind voiced the question. Words were not needed in this place.

"You are home," said a soothing voice. Vaguely he thought the voice sounded like his mother, Judith, but deeper and warmer somehow.

"How did I get here?"

"It has been a long journey. Now you can rest."

"I can't rest." The thought was reaction, unconscious. His conscious mind wanted nothing more than to rest here, to fade away into this ocean of calm.

"Yes you can."

"No." He was sure this time and suddenly the warm light changed; became less welcoming and sharper somehow.

"Then you have made the right choice Michael Smith," said the voice and now Michael understood that it was his mother, Lillian, speaking to him. He opened his eyes and found himself in a small room. The room was quiet and peaceful; not the same as the light but peaceful still.

Morning sun rays glinted in through the open window and the walls were covered with paintings of trees and bright green fields. Michael recognized this place.

"Hello Michael." The woman sat to his right upon the soft bed. "It is so good to see you again." The light fell upon her face in a bright cascade and Michael had to squint to really make out her features.

"Mom," he said, smiling. His mind did not question the impossibility of her presence; it simply accepted it and moved on.

"You have done so much. You have done so well. But your journey is not yet finished."

"I know. I have to stop Allcraft."

"Yes."

Suddenly the room was swept away and it vanished, replaced by a hillside cliff overlooking a bright blue ocean. Michael stood just at the edge of the cliff, looking down the long distance to the cresting waves. Lillian stood by his side, her white gown flowing in the cool breeze.

"This was the hardest day of my life," said Lillian, gazing toward the horizon. "I had to lay your father to rest here."

"I know," said Michael. "I was here; hiding like a coward."

Lillian smiled at her son. "No Michael. It took great courage to come here," she said. "It was here I hid what Allcraft seeks with such passion. The one thing you must not allow him to have."

"The book? The words to fill it?" said Michael, calmly looking over the cliff at the waves. Lillian nodded. "But I have the book," said Michael, holding out his hand. He offered the book to his mother. "It was hidden in Treasure Island. Remember when you used to read that to me?"

"Yes, of course Michael. The book is blank now. I hid the words," said Lillian.

"Hid them? Where?"

"Here. In this place. Look," said Lillian, pointing to the sea below. As Michael watched, a small white ball emerged from beneath the waves and rose up toward them. "I had to hide them here, on that day. Michael, Allcraft cannot have this book. With this and with the power he has accumulated he will have free reign to destroy Earth and recreate it in his image. This cannot happen."

"I know," said Michael, watching the white ball rise up and ever closer.

"It is more dire than you think Michael. Earth and Serafina are connected; they are twins. If one dies, the other dies. Earth is not merely a Fabrication; it is the other side of the coin." Michael smiled for a moment and thought of the coin his mother gave him so long ago, in the same canyon where he now stood. Only he wasn't in Couplet Canyon, he was here, with her.

"They are connected," she said, the white ball getting closer and closer, glowing in the sunlight. "They must coexist."

Now the ball was in front of them, hovering just out of reach. Michael watched as the ball grew brighter and brighter until it was gone.

"Now look," said Lillian, her eyes moving to the book in Michael's hand.

He opened the tome and watched as the ball of light floated toward the opened book, landed and disappeared. Michael blinked, the light bright for a moment. When he looked again at the pages before him, spidery letters and words filled the pages.

"This is the Song of the Seraphim. This is the text the Seraphim used to create Earth. Only with its power can one hope to create an entire world. I entrust this power to you now, my son."

Michael, hypnotized, gazed at the cover of the book and watched as an ornate symbol, silver and gold, emblazoned itself on the cover. A gold snake wound its way around a silver tree branch; from the snake's open mouth sprung another snake which wound around and connected to the fist snake at its tail.

"The symbol of the Seraphim. My ancestors; your ancestors." Lillian smiled. "I have to leave you now Michael. You are strong, but you must rely on your sister as well. Mya is the key to all of this and you both have a part to play."

Michael remembered his mother holding his hand before she closed her eyes for the last time, remembered her words: *I hid the stone somewhere only you can go, a place filled with light.* Michael understood now; he understood about the Departure, how his mother used all her power cull the words from the book, hide them here and keep them safe for him, for this moment.

"Mom . . . I love you."

Lillian did not reply, only smiled and was gone, leaving Michael alone on the cliffside, the sound of the distant waves crashing below. He looked down at the Song of the Seraphim, at the ornate symbol staring back up at him. Then the scene changed once more. The ocean and the cliffs withdrew and left Michael standing at the foot of a massive, wooden roller coaster. An amusement park sprawled out around him but he was the only patron.

"We were gonna' go here before you vanished that day in your mother's hospital room, remember?" For a second, only a second, Michael did not place the voice. Then it was clear. He spun around and standing before him Michael saw his Dad.

"Dad!" He shouted.

"Hey son. Long time no see," said Peter Smith, smiling. A wellspring of emotions flooded into Michael; regret, sadness and joy.

"How are you here?" said Michael.

"Because of you. You are making this all happen right now. I guess your mind connected with the Twinning and here we are."

"I miss you dad," said Michael.

"I miss you too. You're so much older," said Peter, smiling.

"No more hamburger helper I guess?" Michael laughed. "Are you going to make it Michael? Can you make it?"

"I don't know Dad. I want to but I just don't know."

"Well know this. I believe in you. You have become a great man Michael, capable of anything. I know you will see this thing through."

Michael could feel tears forming in his eyes.

"Thanks Dad. I won't forget this."

"Do you know where Allcraft is now?"

"I'm not sure."

"He's close. You should have no trouble finding him. He is connected to the Twinning now too. Think of it like a compass and he's north. The Twinning will show you the way."

"Okay," said Michael.

"And you have the book?"

Michael nodded, and held up the Song of the Seraphim.

"And you have Mya?"

Michael nodded again.

"Then you have all that you need. Meet me back here some time and we can ride that," said Peter as a car swooshed down the drop of the roller coaster.

"I will dad."

"You have to go now Michael. You have to stop him."

"I will."

"Good. Take care, kiddo."

Michael nodded and watched as, once again, the scene before him vanished and he found himself in darkness, alone. He heard the sound of an industrial light clunk on and a red door stood before him, bathed in a spotlight. He walked toward the red door, prepared for what he might find on the other side. He could feel his soul shivering and every fiber of his being resonating with the Twinning. He reached out for the door's handle and turned it. The door opened slowly and Michael walked through.

▼

CHAPTER 21

CYRIL'S GIFT

"This plan is ludicrous," said Ja'Mirra, storming across the room, her feet sloughing across the animal fur rug on the floor. "Not even Lillian VanVargott was that powerful."

"It doesn't matter Fabricantress," said Lucas Allcraft, paying special attention to add some extra venom to the formal name for Ja'Mirra's order. She glared at him, her face still red and splotchy in places, but her eyes still burning with the same fury they always had.

"How can you hope to create an entire world for yourself?" From the window came the sound of screams and, in the distance, the distinct noise of splintering wood.

"Because of this," said Allcraft, presenting the jewel around his neck, "and because of them." He pointed toward the sleeping figures in the corner of the room, nestled by the fire. They were not, however, sleeping. "And because nothing can stop us now. The Seraphim sing no more. Their mighty creation," he said, lifting his hand toward the window, "is falling apart. It is a new world Ja'Mirra," he said, moving toward her. "Stand by my side . . . or don't." His eyes glared, the fire sending fragments of slanting light across them.

"I'm with you," she said, her chest heaving beneath her blue, gossamer gown.

"Good. Come." Grabbing her hand, Allcraft pulled her from the room and led her down the hallway of the house they currently occupied. The front room was filled with Bargouls of all shapes and sizes; some blue and green, others tan and purple. At the sight of Allcraft, several of them jumped to attention and a few even buzzed up to the ceiling.

"Randall," said Allcraft. One of the Bargouls moved toward Allcraft.

"Yes, Master."

"Is it done?"

"Nearly sire. The town is ours; the residents are either fleeing or dead; your creatures saw to that."

"Good. And what about the Overpower?"

"Dead."

Allcraft smiled. One more King dethroned. There would be only chaos when he was finished with Serafina; a world ready for the taking. And Earth; a world ready to be shaped in the image of Lucas Allcraft. "Then none remain. Serafina burns around us, its Kings dethroned. Ja'Mirra, would you like to rule one of the Overpowers?"

"Lucas, surely you can't be . . ."

"But I am. You have served me well Ja'Mirra. You even came back to me after I betrayed you. For that, you have earned a just reward. Name your new Barony."

Ja'Mirra thought for a moment; back to when she was a young girl. Memories of the sea, of her parents and the warmth of the sun on her skin.

"Hapmarcom then, by the sea."

"Done," said Allcraft smiling. The door to the house opened and, through the archway, Bartlebug appeared.

"Bartlebug, just in time. When I leave this place, you may have Blanchfield. It is yours."

If Bargouls could smile, Bartlebug would have smiled deeply at this news. After all his loyal service his master had given him something he had always wished for.

"Yes master, thank you."

Allcraft nodded. "Now go, secure the rest of the townsfolk and make sure they do not return."

"Actually master that is why I came back. One of them wishes to speak with you."

Allcraft raised an eyebrow, curious at the request.

"Bring him then," said Allcraft.

"It is a woman sire," replied Bartlebug.

"Then send her, and be quick about it!"

Bartlebug rapped on the door and again it opened, this time a young girl, no more than eighteen, came through the door. Her face was dirty and her clothes torn in places. A few bloody scratches could be seen on her body in various spots. Ja'Mirra recognized her instantly.

"Cyril?" she said. "I haven't seen you since . . ."

"Since that night when you decided to live again, headmistress," said Cyril, cutting her off.

"Well what are you doing here, then?" demanded Allcraft.

"This Barony, Bouresque, is . . . was my home. And you have destroyed it," said Cyril, eyes glaring. She glanced to her sides, very aware of the massive presence of the Bargouls surrounding her.

"Indeed I have. I am your new ruler. This world is mine," replied Allcraft, smirking.

Cyril remained silent, then spoke.

"I helped Ja'Mirra bring you back two years ago at the Cerulean School. I also helped Michael Smith try to stop that from happening. I have fought against your creatures to try and save the place I was born, the place I call home. I have used my powers of the Fabricant to try and stop you. But I have failed." Allcraft smiled, his sinister teeth barred. "But he will not," said Cyril, looking directly at Allcraft.

For a moment, Allcraft's eyes flickered, but only for a fleeting moment.

"What do you want Fabricantress?" demanded Allcraft, temper rising.

"Only one thing." Quickly, Cyril reached into the folds of her gown, the motion raising alarm among the Bargouls, many of whom protruded their stings and rushed towards her.

"Here," she said, producing an object from her gown.

"And what is this?" said Allcraft, moving one step closer to examine the object.

"All I have left to give."

Ja'Mirra recognized the object instantly but was uncertain if Allcraft knew about Culling Stones. The Stones were ancient and widely thought to be lost forever. Ja'Mirra could not imagine how Cyril could have come to possess one.

"What is it?" said Allcraft. Before Cyril could answer, she smashed the stone into her chest, expelling a loud breath in the process. Suddenly, her body filled with light, shooting at all angles and painting the room in bright waves. The Bargouls screamed, as if in pain, and many of them dropped to the floor in agony. Bartlebug, the closest of all of them to the Culling Stone, was blinded by the light and went crashing backward, toward the door. Allcraft watched as the young girl Cyril rose a few feet off the ground, her body now pouring with white light. Then Cyril spoke for the last time.

"I have given myself up to the Twinning. My corporeal body is no more. My final wish; to mark this man. Mark this man with the light of the Fabricant so that, even in darkness, he shall be found." Her voice echoed off the walls of the house, reverberating across the hallways and out to the town. From Cyril's body a shaft of light shot at Allcraft who did not have time to move from its path. The light penetrated him and he screamed out; more in rage than in pain, and dropped to his knees. He looked up, and watched as Cyril's body grew brighter and brighter until, in one final blast of vibrant light, she was gone.

Allcraft growled at Ja'Mirra, "What was that?"

"A Culling Stone," replied Ja'Mirra. "Just like the one you have there around your neck." Allcraft glanced down at the stone around his neck, the heirloom given to him so long ago; red and dimly glowing. The other had been white and pure. "I'm surprised you didn't recognize it given you have one," said Ja'Mirra, incredulously. Allcraft ignored her. "She used her Ember to mark you. I think you know quite well who received the other end of that mark."

"Smith," said Allcraft. Ja'Mirra nodded. Allcraft rose from his knees, looking around at the dazed Bargouls. "So what does that mean?"

"It means he can use the Twinning to find you. He will find you no matter where you go."

Allcraft chuckled. "Let him come. He is already too late. Bartlebug!" shouted Allcraft. He did not receive a reply. "Bartlebug, come here!" Allcraft looked toward the door of the house and saw a Bargoul lying by the wall, not moving. Allcraft moved closer. "Bartlebug?" he said. At last the Bargoul stirred, barely moving. His wings buzzed feebly, unable to carry him from the floor.

"I am . . . alright," he said, staggering to his feet. "That light . . ."

"We are leaving," commanded Allcraft. "Gather Lucious and Lavinia." The Bargouls followed the command

and the group made their way from the borrowed home of one of Hapmarcom's most successful and well-liked shop keepers, Walter Umby. His body lay silent on the bed in the upstairs room. With the burning Barony of Hapmarcom at their backs, Allcraft and his followers made their way to the place where everything ended, the final destination he had imagined for all these years; his moment of triumph at hand.

Chapter 22

▼

Another Compass

Michael awoke to the sound of crickets; far away but present, their rhythmic chirping softening the evening air. Before opening his eyes he felt the soft brush of cool grass upon his cheek, heard the bubbling sound of an unseen brook close by and eddying into distant and unknown paths. As he listened to the crickets he wondered, for a moment, if he was back home; a boy lying on the grass, listening to the verdant summer evening as the sun went down and his parents prepared dinner inside. He wondered if crickets even existed in Serafina; it would seem they did, or at least something that sounded just like them. He listened only a moment more and then opened his eyes.

The sun had just set beyond the horizon and a faint trace of light still lingered, casting eerie and at the same time incredibly peaceful shadows all around him. On Earth they called this twilight. Getting to his knees he realized the book his mother had hidden for him to find was still in his hand only now the cover, once only a tattered brown skin, was now covered in flittering gold regalia, spidery lines weaving in and out, all connected to the central symbol of the snake, writhing in an unending circle, consuming its own tail. He opened the book, about half way, and began reading in the dim light still pouring from above.

"*This great journey, this wonderful act, shall always set us apart from everyone who came before us,*" he read aloud, his voice alone among the crickets, "*and through this great act we shall always linger in the hearts of our people. We sacrifice ourselves for this willingly, joyfully. This, above all else, is the most high and noble act we can begin and this sacrifice becomes the essential symbol for the world we shall create. Without sacrifice, without willingly laying down one's own life, there can be no salvation and no hope of success.*" Michael closed the book.

His mind wandered for a moment, reflecting on the words. All those who had died since this journey began; his own father and mother, countless innocents, friends. Michael wondered if they died for something noble and high or for something vein, something greedy and petty like the will of Lucas Allcraft. As he thought, Michael noticed night falling all around him, the sun had fully set in the few moments he was reading from the book; the book now filled page to page with words, scrawled in spidery calligraphy and intricately winding across each page. For some reason Michael opened the book once more and this time, in the darkness, flipped to the back. At the end a large section of the book was blank; the words stopped about mid way through one of the pages and the rest were empty. He read the final sentence in the very last slant of light:

"*And now you shall command the Twinning for us and from a new lineage will spring, a new hope, a new world.*" And then the words stopped.

Michael once more closed the book but this time, now standing in full dark, he noticed something odd. The book shimmered and gave off an iridescent, soft glow. He held the tome up and examined, confirming his observations. Indeed, the glow seemed to ebb and flow around the book.

Then, Michael noticed a single point of light, jutting from the back cover of the book. As he turned to look at it, Michael realized the point was fixed and no matter which way he turned the book, the point of light continued pointing in the same direction.

"It's like a compass," he said. His mind jittered softly, back to a foggy memory of another compass, one very different from the light coming from the book.

Then, after a few moments thought, he said, "Allcraft."

Somehow, Michael knew the book was showing him the way to find Allcraft and to stop his madness at long last. To set right the wrongs Michael had so willingly unleashed upon these two worlds and to save what little hope remained for each.

Tucking the Song of the Seraphim into his belt and making sure it was tight, Michael took one last look at the point of light coming from the book and, cocking his head toward the sky, rose from the ground and shot into the dark heavens. The light from the book was enough to guide him as he flew, silently over the landscape. He wasn't sure where the Couplet Canyon portal had dropped him, but he knew where he needed to go and he soared, flew as fast as he could under the white moon, toward his destiny.

CHAPTER 23

VOICES FROM BEYOND

Mya's thoughts rested solely on Michael. Now, with the Mayweathers gone, her friends buried and Luscious and Lavinia lost to the dark feints of Lucas Allcraft, Mya could do nothing but think about her next step. She sat, silently, upon a piece of what had been Quixitix' home. The fires had been put out and all signs of the ghastly Twilight monsters were gone. The sun was just setting beyond the far hills as Mya gazed at it, watched it slowly lower itself beyond the furthest mound. She wondered where Michael had gone since they split off in town; if he was drawing in on Allcraft now and how he would be able to fight the Magican by himself.

"I never should have let him go," she said softly, shaking her head. Her long, blond hair fell around her in waves and as she sat on the cobblestone thinking, she realized what she needed to do. "I won't leave you Michael." And so she set off, not knowing where to go or what she would find when she got there, but following whatever fate or destiny had led her to this point.

The night expanded around her as she walked, not sure of the direction but following something inside her. She knew Michael had the book, and that was good, but she also knew that without her help he might not survive the confrontation with Allcraft. From time to time Mya tuned in to the sound of her footsteps; sometimes on gravel, the crunching of each press, and sometimes on the dirt, the soft whisper of warm ground. In the distance a wild coyote or some such creature howled at the now hanging moon, white and vibrant and calling her forward. She became lost in her thoughts as she walked. She thought about all those she had lost, people she had failed to protect. Dunny and Quixitix; gone forever. The innocent twins Lucious and Lavinia; she had failed to save them. Her mother. Her father. Michael.

As if in response to her thoughts Mya felt something well up inside her. She stopped, and listened for a moment, feeling her heart quicken. Suddenly, the night was broken by a shaft of brilliant light, a tower of luminous brightness standing in front of her. Mya had never seen anything like it before. She stared at the tower of light, mesmerized. For a moment she thought it was a dream or some kind of hallucination; perhaps she had fallen asleep as she walked. She had no idea where she was or how far she had traveled in the few short hours of her nighttime wandering, but standing before the tower of light, Mya felt she was in the right place. Then she heard it.

Starting very softly, like quiet footsteps, Mya began to hear singing coming from the light. At first she was sure it was her mind playing tricks on her but as she listened she realized it was real and it was coming from just in front of her, flowing from this shaft of light.

She spoke the words without thinking, the power of the music compelling her, "it's so beautiful." Indeed, Mya had never heard anything like it before; notes and tones her ears had never experienced. The melody and the voices, all in unison, created a wave of sound and it flooded over Mya. From the corners of her eyes a few tears formed, an involuntary reaction to hearing the Song of the Seraphim for the first time.

"Mya VanVargott," spoke a voice from the light. To Mya, the voice sounded unmistakably like Lillian. "You are the last of our kind and so we come to you now in our most dire hour. Never before have we intervened with the course of the world but we need you now as we never have before." The voice hovered and echoed around Mya.

"The last of your kind? What do you mean?"

"You are the last descendant of the Seraphim. Your mother, Lillian, was a Seraphim. Her mother, and her mother tracing back to the start of time. Our blood flows in you now and we call upon you here to thwart the menace trying to destroy our most beloved creation."

"Earth?" said Mya.

"Yes. We created Earth out of love, a place where people could be free, a new world. We never knew what would become of our creation. Some things we are pleased with, others we are not." Mya listened, intently, unable to look away from the shaft of light. "But now the Magican Lucas Allcraft threatens our creation and only you can stop him. Allcraft has already silenced too many of us and Earth can no longer persist without us. He has taken our power and he will use it."

"What about Michael? He can wield both the Fabricant and the Magicant. If he can't stop Allcraft . . ."

"Michael Smith has a role to play in the end and he will succeed. But he cannot do what must, ultimately, be done Mya. That responsibility lies with you."

"What do you mean?" she asked.

"Come Mya, come into the light and we will help you one last time. The rest of your journey belongs to you. We know you will make the right choice when the time comes; for all of us." The voice faded away and the singing stopped.

Mya rose to her feet, staring at the shaft of light. Slowly, she approached it. She could feel the warmth it gave off, like a ray of sunlight on her shoulders, and it reminded her of the field of roses she played in as a girl. An endless field of red stretching out to the horizon; the field she had first seen Michael in, sitting upon an old tree stump. She reached out and touched the light and both the tower of light and Mya vanished in an instant, leaving only the distant sound of a baying coyote and the stark white moon looking down on the spot where moments before she had stood.

From the *Song of the Seraphim*

Chapter 10, Verse 17

. . . for it is unto the world we give ourselves and our sacrifice, our lives and our lineage, our faith and our hope. We must look past ourselves, look past our own desires and wishes and look only toward a bright future. A future full of hope, of life and of love. Without these things, all is lost.

Chapter 24

▼

Together Again

In an instant, Mya was transported a great distance, giving her no time at all to react. Her body, carried along by the flow and ebb of the Twinning, materialized near a few lonesome trees and several large rocks. Night still conquered the landscape and Mya could not see very far around her so she did not know where she had been taken. In the distance a large structure loomed before her, a few torches flickering from tall parapets. Suddenly she heard some voices behind her, a little ways off but approaching her arrival spot. Quickly, Mya ducked behind one of the larger rocks and made sure she was not visible to the approaching travelers. She waited and listened as they passed.

"He says this is it then, this is the end a'the road."

Along with their voices, Mya also heard an unmistakable buzzing sound; she knew that sound anywhere. The Bargouls continued talking.

"So what then eh? What happens once he's won?"

"You remember the ancient tales right? The way we was treated back then, by 'im no less, his own personal guards and such. Treated as equals, given whatever 'are little heart's desire."

"Sounds nice."

Mya listened and watched as they passed her, one of them carrying a small torch, the light illuminating the path before them. The dirt road and slightly swaying tall grass became washed in the waves of the torchlight and the Bargouls' faces, sooty black through and through, were momentarily illuminated in each bob up and down.

"Word is he's ready; whatever that means," said the first one.

"Soon then?"

"Aye, soon, soon. Allcraft's a good man. We would still be dust in the ground if not 'fer 'im."

The name struck Mya, her mind racing, hoping the Seraphim had brought her to where she needed to be, had brought her to Allcraft's doorstep. Eventually the Bargouls were out of ear shot and heading toward the large castle in the distance. She waited several minutes and then stood up, scanning her surroundings. Nothing, she was alone. She looked at the castle and imagined Allcraft sitting in there somewhere, high up in one of the towers, waiting for the moment to unleash his will upon the Twinning and destroy what was left of Earth. She imagined Lucious and Lavinia in there as well, cowering and scared, hungry, thirsty, probably hurt. The Seraphim had delivered her to this place for a reason and although Mya did not know what role she would play in the events to come, she knew one thing for certain; she needed to find her way into that castle and stop Allcraft.

Her mind made up, Mya stepped from behind the boulder and quietly set off on the dirt path. As soon as she took her first step she heard a noise, almost inaudible, from behind her and she spun around, realizing it was too late to hide and ready for a fight. Nothing there, just the empty path. She heard the noise again, to her left this time and she thought she saw something move in the trees.

"Mya!" said a voice from the brush. She could not see the owner of the voice but she saw some bushes rustle and a figure emerge.

"Michael!" she shouted, rushing toward him. They embraced, for just a moment, and then Michael spoke.

"The Seraphim brought you here, didn't they?" said Michael.

Mya looked at him, moonlight illuminating her features. "How did you know?"

"Because of this," he said.

From his belt Michael produced the book and Mya stared at it, watching the glowing light pulsate and the point of light stick out, facing directly at the castle ahead.

"Look inside," said Michael. "It's filled with words. This is the real thing Mya."

Mya opened the book and scanned the pages, reading a few words here and there.

"Michael, did you notice the end was blank? Why are these pages here?"

Michael looked at her intently. "I don't know. But I think this book is the key. I'm not sure how or why, but we will need it in the end."

Mya handed the book back to Michael and he placed it securely back into his belt.

"He's in there," he said.

"Yes," said Mya.

They stood silent for a moment, looking at the tall castle before them, both of them wondering what they would find inside.

"We made it here together Mya. The Seraphim helped us. They want us to stop him, to save these worlds. At least we have that," said Michael. Mya nodded.

"Michael I have to tell you something . . ." said Mya, preparing to deliver the sad news about Dunny and Quixitix. Michael looked at her, determined and hardened, prepared for the struggle ahead. "I will be with you. Always." She would tell him . . . some other time.

Michael smiled, something he rarely did these days, and in the darkness outside of Allcraft's castle, for the first time, Michael felt good. He took Mya's hand, squeezed it, and then let it go.

Together they walked, quickly, down the dirt path; following behind the two Bargouls Mya had seen on patrol earlier. Eventually they caught up to the Bargouls and silently subdued them, hiding their unconscious bodies behind rocks on the side of the road. Soon, they stood at the base of the massive tower and gazed up at it.

Michael once again took Mya's hand and embraced her. Then, together, they rose up through the air, the power of the Magicant carrying them upward, the landscape falling away beneath them. Quietly, Michael landed at the top of the parapet on a small outcropping. He noticed a wooden door leading inside and made his way to it with Mya behind him. They silently opened the door and entered the tower.

CHAPTER 25

▼

JA'MIRRA

The castle was unguarded, as far as Michael and Mya could tell, at least from this uppermost entry point. Perhaps several Bargouls or other foul creations of Allcraft's patrolled the grounds and floors below, but Michael assumed Allcraft did not have the foresight to post any sort of guard in the tiny room at the top of the tower. The room they entered was small and contained only a few obscure items; a desk, a wooden chest and a few small candles burning towards the end of their wicks. Michael and Mya crept through the room slowly, making as little noise as possible, until they found a slender staircase leading down. Mya went first this time, bowing low as she descended the stairs in order to see if anyone inhabited the room below. No one did and the duo continued their infiltration of the castle. This lower room, carpeted and more heavily furnished, had a small fireplace tucked away in one corner with a few sparse embers still burning from a fire that was there before. This room contained two doors; one large and wooden, the other small and made of hard metal.

"Which door?" whispered Mya. Michael motioned toward the larger, wooden door and they made their way toward it. The door opened without a sound and beyond it a snaking hallway greeted them. For a moment Michael's mind raced back to the first time he ever found himself inside Blanchfield Castle; the red carpet and torches snaking their way around odd corners, the first time he bumped into Dunny. This hallway closely resembled that one. Before they proceeded, Michael pulled the book from his belt and consulted the point of light. It pointed straight ahead, telling him this hallway was the way to go. He secured the book and they proceeded.

Halfway down the hallway they began to hear voices and, at times, shouts. They slowly crept along the stone wall and eventually wound around a lazy corner. There, they found a door, half open, and the voices emanating from within.

"Are you sure you are alright? You have been acting strange ever since the incident with that girl," said one voice, a woman's.

"Yes. I am fine," said the other voice. Michael recognized it immediately and from the look on Mya's face she did too; Bartlebug. "I just feel . . . I don't know," said Bartlebug from within the room. Michael and Mya continued to listen from just outside the door.

"So what do you think of your new appointment?" said the woman's voice. Mya knew she recognized who the voice belonged to but she could not pinpoint it.

"It's fine. I suppose I have earned it. Not much left to rule now though; we will certainly be starting from scratch."

"Better to rule here than to serve there I suppose," said the woman. Finally, Mya realized who the woman was.

"Ja'Mirra . . ." Bartlebug trailed off.

"Yes?" replied Ja'Mirra from inside the room.

For a moment no sound came from the room and Michael and Mya wondered what had happened. Finally, Bartlebug spoke.

"You know I am loyal to Master Allcraft," said the Bargoul.

"Of course I know that. As am I," replied Ja'Mirra.

"Indeed. Well, our Master has tasked me with a final job and that is why I have come here tonight. I must ask you a question."

"A question?" said Ja'Mirra. Michael thought he heard a twinge of fear in the Fabricantress' voice.

"Would you mind?" said Bartlebug. For a few moments no one spoke, and then the Bargoul asked his question. "When, precisely, were you planning on betraying Master Allcraft?"

Michael and Mya looked at each other, fearfully. Before they could say or do anything they heard a muffled scream come from the room followed by a loud thud.

"He never trusted you," said Bartlebug. Michael and Mya pressed themselves against the wall as they realized the Bargoul was approaching the half-opened door, about to leave the room. If he turned right he would bump directly into them; they could only hope he turned left.

Holding their breath and remaining as still as possible, they waited for the few agonizing seconds before Bartlebug emerged and either found them or missed them completely. Then, Bartlebug made his exit, walking on his padded feet, slowly, looking down at the ground, mumbling to himself. Turning to his left, Michael and Mya stood stone-still as the Bargoul made his way down the hallway away from them, through another door, and then he was gone. They let out a saved breath and rushed into the room.

In the flickering candlelight Michael and Mya saw the body of Ja'Mirra sprawled on the floor, her blue gown quickly becoming damp with her own blood. A massive wound spread from the small of her back; a barbed puncture from Bartlebug's stinger. Michael rushed to her, already knowing it was too late. He turned her over and she winced, her face pale and her eyes bloodshot. Michael saw for the first time the damage left by the vicious attack Allcraft gave her in the Culling Chamber years ago; scars and puffy white tissue stood out all over her face. She opened her eyes.

"You," she said. "You're here." Her voice sounded far off and distant.

"I'm sorry," said Michael. "Too many have been lost already." Mya knelt next to them and looked at the former Headmistress of the Cerulean School, a woman Mya had once regarded with great respect and admiration, now dying on the floor in a pool of her own blood. Mya didn't know what to feel; her emotions tangled in pity, anger and cold finality.

"The necklace," she said. "The power of the Seraphim is in the necklace, it is a Culling Stone." Ja'Mirra coughed and a small rivulet of blood formed at the corner of her mouth. "This is the end," she said. She smiled, weakly, and looked directly at both of them. "I'm sorry." And then she was gone. Michael gently placed her body back on the ground.

"There was nothing we could do," he said to Mya. Upset, she nodded.

"All this killing . . . all this suffering," said Mya. "For what? Why does the world have to be so cruel?"

"It doesn't," said Michael. "It is the choices we make that shape the world. We have that power." Mya nodded. Michael thought for a moment about the sacred object his mother had told him about as she lay dying, the stone she used to cull the words from the pages of the book he now held. He turned to his sister.

"Have you ever heard of Culling Stones? What can you tell me about them?"

Mya thought for a moment. "Mother used to speak of them, but not very often. Ancient objects, thought to no longer exist. They are said to channel the power of the Twinning and funnel it into whoever wields the stone."

"If Allcraft has one . . ." Michael's mind raced, struggling to put the pieces together. Then it clicked. "That's what I was destroying . . . all those times, the Seraphim. He told me they were just lifeless husks. All those red jewels . . . they were these Culling Stones. He must have one of his own and now . . ."

"That must be how he sent those creatures," said Mya. They looked at each other.

"Let's go," said Michael.

They rushed from the room and down the hallway, leaving the lifeless body of Lady Ja'Mirra behind. Eventually they reached the door Bartlebug had used earlier and passed through it, totally unaware of what waited for them on the other side.

CHAPTER 26

▼

ALLCRAFT'S PLAN

The room sprawled out before them; massive and dimly lit. Circular in shape, the walls curved in parabolic arches on both sides and ornate candelabras stood like flickering sentinels jutting from the stone. As Michael and Mya stepped into the room the first thing their eyes settled on caused them to lose their breath; in the center of the circular expanse a mound rose from the floor; it looked like dirt. Atop this mound, bound and suspended from the room's ceiling and hanging like a dangling branch, was Lucious. He was badly beaten and his eyes were closed. The light from the circular walls cast odd shadows on the boy as he slowly spun above the dirt. Michael and Mya could not see beyond the dirt mound to the other side of the room but despite this they rushed forward to help their friend.

"Lucious!" screamed Michael, running toward the dirt hill. It was taller than it looked when they had first entered the room and now they both started to climb it, their feet sticking into the damp soil. "Lucious can you hear me?" said Mya, clawing her way to the top of the mound.

At last they reached the top and found shoddy footholds in the dirt, sending pieces of dusky debris falling down around them. Michael summoned the Magicant and with a quick swipe of his hand he burned through the rope holding

226

Lucious up. Lucious fell and Mya caught his body, sending them both falling to the dirt.

"Lucious, Lucious!" said Mya, wiping the grime and blood away from his face. "Are you alright?" Finally Lucious stirred and, with struggle, opened his eyes.

"Mya," he said.

"I think he's . . ." said Mya, looking at Michael, but before she could finish the sentence, a large patch of dirt exploded beside her, sending her crashing, rolling, down the hill. Lucious went rolling down the opposite side of the mound and Michael watched, helpless. Then another patch of dirt exploded and Michael barely had time to avoid the blast, jumping to his right and rolling. He almost lost his footing and fell down the hill but caught himself at the last moment. With a quick glance he saw Mya lying at the foot of the hill, unmoving.

"Welcome Magican!" said a voice from the darkness, loud and hissing.

"Allcraft!" shouted Michael, and he took to the air, not sure how much vertical space he had. He quickly found he did not have much as he slammed into the stone ceiling, hard. His head hurt for a moment, then he moved as another explosion rocked the stone around him and a few pieces fell nearby.

"This certainly feels familiar!" shouted the voice. "Only this time, you will lose!"

Michael zoomed around the circular room, looking for the source of the voice, keeping the dirt mound to his right as he circled. No more explosions came for a few moments and Michael decided to land and check on Mya. He found her quickly and landed next to her.

"Mya, Mya wake up!" he said. She opened her eyes, dazed only for a moment, and then she snapped back to reality.

"Come on Mya," said Michael, pulling her to her feet. "Allcraft is here," he said. Together they ran around the dirt mound until they found Lucious, breathing but unconscious, at the foot of the mound on the opposite side.

"Grab his legs," said Michael. Mya complied and they moved Lucious away from the mound and against one of the stone walls underneath the flickering candle light.

"He's here, somewhere Mya."

"Alright," she said, ready. They waited, a few moments, listening to the sound of their breathing and the crackle of the fire above them. Then the room exploded.

The mound of dirt erupted from within, sending a rain of warm, damp soil everywhere in the room. A few terrible moments passed during which Michael and Mya could see nothing in the torrent of dirt; by the end Lucious was nearly covered in it. Then they saw what the dirt had been concealing.

In the center of the room, now visible, hovered a rift, a tear in the fabric of the world. Somehow Allcraft had covered it with a mound of dirt but now the rift was exposed and Michael and Mya had never seen anything like it before. It glowed with the deepest and truest colors either of them had ever seen; undulating like a snake and flowing like a river at the same time. The rift was massive but not the biggest either of them had seen. It was, however, the most pure, the most potent and Mya quickly realized why this rift was here and why it was so important.

"This is the source," said Mya. "This must have been one of the first tears they made, the Seraphim," she said.

"So then this is where he will start," said Michael.

"Very good children!" said Allcraft, emerging from behind the rift. He was dressed in all black and his hair hung straight down; a few strands stood up and were being pulled toward the rift; the silver streak still ran straight down the center of his mane. "Only I think you both still don't quite grasp the seriousness of your situation."

From the other side of the rift the familiar form of Bartlebug, hovering in the air, emerged. They closed in on Michael and Mya. As they got closer, Michael noticed a small string around Allcraft's neck; he could not see the stone, but he figured it was there.

"It's over Allcraft. This is the end. You have done enough," shouted Mya.

"I really don't think so Mya. This is the beginning!"

"We will stop you," said Michael, his eyes shooting back and forth between Allcraft and Bartlebug.

"Nope," said Allcraft. "You see, it's already done. All that time together Smith, you already sealed the fate of your own world. Thank you for that, by the way."

Allcraft's words incited Michael further and he could feel the Magicant bubbling up inside him, he could visualize the fire, blue and pure, engulfing Allcraft once and for all.

"Oh, I see. You certainly are an amateur. Did I ever tell you that Smith?" Allcraft made a quick motion with his hand and suddenly Michael felt nothing; the fire was gone.

"What did you do!" he demanded.

"You think you know how to wield that power boy! I have been studying it and using it my whole life; for one hundred years I was bound to a book in Twilight and still I honed my skills, let the Magicant take me over. You, Smith, know not what you do."

With a quick movement of his hand Allcraft summoned the Magicant and suddenly Michael felt as if he was choking; he could not breathe. He opened his mouth and water began gushing onto the floor, mixing with the displaced dirt and creating a slippery, muddy surface.

"Mya," he gurgled, his voice barely heard. Water continued to pour from his mouth, an endless river blocking his wind pipe.

"Michael!" shouted Mya, and without thinking, the Fabricant was there for her. Quicker than Allcraft could anticipate, a massive white fist, made entirely of light, appeared and slammed into Allcraft, sending him flying through the air toward the rift. Before he crashed into it he righted himself, midair, and glared at Mya. In the split second his guard was down, the water stopped flowing from Michael's throat long enough for him to catch his breath. His mind raced and then he felt electric; he could feel a surge of something tingling and rising up to the surface. Allcraft noticed this change but it was too late. From the ceiling a massive grey cloud appeared from thin air and from this cloud, several bolts of lightning rained down. Allcraft flew about the room, dodging them. The last bolt connected and sent Allcraft smashing into the far wall. Michael relaxed for a moment and looked for Bartlebug. He did not see the Bargoul.

"Watch out for Bartlebug Mya," said Michael, his throat still raspy from the water.

"There!" Mya shouted, pointing behind Michael. From the shadows, the Bargoul came at them fast, yelling. Michael summoned wind, felt it surge inside him and with a swipe of his hand, sent the Bargoul flying off course and toward the rift. He watched and listened as Bartlebug shouted and attempted to regain control of his flight path, but it was too late. Michael and Mya watched the massive bee struggle and then crash into the rift. In a flash of light he was gone; pulled into the Twinning.

While they were distracted, Allcraft moved to the other side of the room and this time he rushed them, flying as fast as he could, directly at them. Michael had no time to react;

all he could do was push Mya out of the way. She yelled as he pushed her, falling to the floor. Allcraft connected, hard, with Michael's body and the impact sent the book from Michael's belt crashing to the floor. Allcraft did not see it fall but instead focused on gripping Michael Smith, hard, and not letting go.

"Now we finish this Smith!" shouted Allcraft, and changed course. Michael had only moments to realize they were now flying straight toward the rift.

"Mya!" shouted Michael, but it was too late. His voice was cut off as Lucas Allcraft and Michael Smith, bound and speeding toward the rift, were both engulfed in Twilight and gone in an instant.

Mya was left alone in the room with Lucious, still breathing but unconscious, and the book; the Song of the Seraphim, resting at her feet. She picked it up and tried to imagine where Michael and Allcraft were, and if she should follow. Then she heard a woman scream.

CHAPTER 27

▼

MICHAEL SMITH

Michael felt the Twinning all around him. It was ever-present and it flowed through him, called to him, and in those first few moments after he and Allcraft entered the rift, the Twinning was all that existed. A pure state of creation and destruction; beginning and end, a force endlessly looping back upon itself, ceasing and starting for eternity.

Pain brought Michael back from that place as his right arm exploded into a wincing, burning source of immense discomfort. He gripped it and realized whatever was hurting him was not coming from an outside source but from within.

"Welcome," said a voice, "to my Twilight. I control this world now and here you are powerless Smith." It was Allcraft. Michael looked around, wincing at the pain in his arm, but saw only endless white. Michael screamed as his other arm flared with the same pain and he dropped to his knees. He looked up and watched as a landscape appeared before him, growing rapidly until it filled his entire viewpoint. Green grass, mountains in the distance and a small sun overhead; Michael thought for a split second he was back on Earth.

"No? How about something else?" said Allcraft, all around him.

The landscape changed instantly around Michael. Now he knelt in a deep snow bank. Ice-capped mountains could barely be seen in the distance as Michael tried to make sense of the scene through a blizzard of snowflakes.

"I could just let you die of cold, but that would be too easy. How about this?"

The ice and snow disappeared and now Michael knelt before a sight he hoped to never encounter again; a massive gingerbread house.

"No," said Michael, reeling from the sight of the place. Suddenly a voice rang out from within the house; a voice dark and terrible and all too familiar.

"Welcome back young Master Smith." It was Smythe, the circus ring leader.

"No!" shouted Michael, terrified.

"No?" said Allcraft, all around him. "Alright. What about this?"

The scene changed again and Michael closed his eyes, refusing to look at whatever horrible scene Allcraft would show him next.

"Look Smith, look at what power I wield!" said Allcraft, jubilant.

Michael kept his eyes firmly closed, refusing to look. Then he felt something inside him; something new; a thought, a small glimmer of realization, an idea that he could manipulate this world too. He opened his eyes.

Before him, just as it had been then, stood his bedroom. The bed, consistently unmade, rested in the far right corner just as he had remembered it as a child. His book shelf, stacked full of his favorite stories, rested right where he remembered and next to it the chair in which his mother would sit and read to him. Spaceman wallpaper, the small, colorful rug in the center, and several shelves lined with stuffed animals, trophies and a few other toys he used to love. The light on his nightstand rotated and cast playful shadows of cats and fish and horses upon the walls. He felt safe. This was his room. Around him, the walls shook briefly, but Michael knew they would hold. He walked to his bed and sat down, comfortable and secure. He felt like he could stay there forever; just sit and start reading his books. He would read them over and over again and he would be happy. He picked one up from the shelf. *Treasure Island*; his favorite. He opened the book to the first page, Chapter 1: *Pieces of Eight.* Just as his eye found the first word on the page, the walls shook again, this time more violently, and before Michael could do anything the wall to his left exploded inward sending rubble all around the room. The bookshelf fell to the floor, spilling his precious books in a pool; he watched as they spread across the floor like liquid.

"You can't hide Smith!" shouted Allcraft. Michael watched through the hole in the wall as creatures came toward him of all shapes and sizes. The sight roused him from his daydream and he stood, his long hair falling around his shoulders, and he left the safety of his room through the newly formed hole.

The first creature came at him with terrible speed, dripping jowls craving a bite of Michael's soft flesh. Michael rose, effortless, into the air and dodged the oncoming creature. As he did, another beast shot at him in mid-air, this one capable of flight. They all bore the same distinct shimmer and flowing, inky skin of creatures born from the Twinning; terrible beasts sent to do Allcraft's dirty work. The aerial creature flew at Michael but with a wave of his hand he sent a ball of blue flame shooting at it and connected, causing the thing to scream and vanish. Michael returned to the ground as more and more creatures came at him. He called upon the wind for some, sending them crashing all around him. Others he drowned with torrents and floods of icy cold water, crashing volumes of liquid down upon their heads and smashing them into the ground. Sometimes he used combinations of elements; wet them first then electrify them, burn them and then send their ashes off in a burst of wind. Allcraft sent creature after creature at Michael Smith and he defeated them all, never tiring. At last, one massive creature strutted toward Michael; it was huge and turtle-like, with razor fangs and several growths sprouting from its back. Its skin shifted and moved with inky, purple sinews.

"Allcraft! Enough! Face me!" shouted Michael. No response. The massive creature moved closer and roared. As it approached Michael realized how tall and towering it really was. He closed his eyes and focused, concentrated. When Michael opened his eyes, his chest exploded with a beam of blue hot fire, aimed directly at the creature. It stood no chance; Michael was too powerful and the beam simply disintegrated the massive beast sending flows of inky Twilight to the ground in all directions.

"Well then," said a voice, this time not all around him but just in front. "I suppose we will have to end this together." Lucas Allcraft materialized in front of Michael and approached. They stood only inches from each other now, Michael nearly as tall as the terrible Magican.

"We have come far together Michael Smith," said Allcraft calmly. "Are you sure you don't wish to come a little further?"

"You're a monster Allcraft. You have betrayed everyone you have ever known. Your greed and avarice will be your destruction and I . . ."

Michael Smith never finished that sentence. As he stared into the eyes of Lucas Allcraft, a sharp and barbed obsidian shaft burst through Michael's chest, cracking bone and piercing flesh. Michael wasn't sure at first what was happening; he felt no pain, just shock. He looked down at his chest and his mind could not comprehend the image he saw there; the black stinger sticking through him, his own blood dripping from it, the smell of hot iron. Allcraft smiled.

"Thank you, Bartlebug for stopping that incessant prattle."

The Bargoul, behind Michael, removed his stinger slowly, savoring the moment. Michael's surprise was only overshadowed by the pain, which came moments after the stinger slid out and flooded his body, but that went away almost immediately.

"I am sorry, Michael Smith. We could have done great things together. But you see, this is not one of your story books."

Michael listened with his last, few remaining moments of life, the world around him fading to black, Allcraft's voice foggy and distant.

"In this story . . . I win."

Michael closed his eyes. He felt warm and happy . . . strange. He could feel the Twinning all around him, cradling him. He thought of home and then he was gone.

Chapter 28

▼

Mya's Journey

Moments after watching her brother and Allcraft disappear into the rift, Mya's chest exploded into agony and she screamed. She could feel something tearing at her from inside, something desperate and wild, clawing and telling her to move. The pain was so great she forgot about the singular scream she heard moments before, the sound registering only for a second and then gone. She staggered, holding her head and her chest, and noticed as she moved toward the rift the pain lessened. She had no idea what to do but she could feel the rift, looming and pulsating, and she gazed at it, transfixed. Then, as if reacting to her stare, the rift reached out for her and Mya vanished. In the same moment Lucious came to and the first thing he saw was Mya being pulled into the rift. He remained now, alone, in the room. The only sound the pulsating of the tear and . . . the woman's scream once more.

"Lavinia!" he shouted. Calling every ounce of his being, Lucious rose from the muddy floor and moved across the room, attempting to locate the source of his sister's screams. "Lavinia!" he shouted again. He had to find her; he would not let anything happen to her.

Stumbling, he made his way down a narrow hallway and found a small room. Leaning against the wall outside the door for a moment, he listened to the voices from inside the room.

"Stop your whelping!" shouted a woman. The voice was followed by a loud slap and Lucious heard Lavinia cry out in pain.

"Please, stop it!" shouted Lavinia.

"You will wait patiently for Master Allcraft and . . ."

Lucious burst into the room, summoning what little strength he had left.

"Stop hurting my sister," he said.

The woman smiled and Lucious recognized her from the most terrible night of his life; it was the Fabricantress from the Culling Chamber.

"Welcome to the party little boy," said Krys. "I hope you enjoy yourself!"

Quicker than he could react, Krys summoned the Fabricant and several tendrils of rope wound themselves around Lucious' body. He could feel the coarse rope burning his skin as it snaked across him and he cried out. Lavinia, although bound, jumped from her spot on the floor and sprinted toward Krys while she focused on Lucious. Krys let out a yell when Lavinia crashed into her and for a moment the ropes loosed enough for Lucious to writhe out of their grasp. Although exhausted, he ran toward Krys, who now rose from the ground.

"Not so fast!" shouted Krys, sending stone pillars rising all around Lucious and trapping him. With a flick of her wrist, Krys bound Lavinia's feet.

"Now you insolent children, we wait for Master Allcraft."

Lucious, exhausted and angry, full of rage and pain, felt something change inside him. He didn't know what it was. He had felt nothing like it before. He gripped his chest and felt something just beneath the surface, rising in him. Krys observed the boy's behavior callously and paid him no mind. Then, Lucious' eyes fixed on Krys, his Ember burning brightly inside them.

"What are you . . ."

Before Krys could finish the sentence, Lucious sent a wave of turquoise fire crashing toward her. She screamed, only for a moment, and then she was gone.

"Lucious . . . that power . . ." said Lavinia. Then Lucious collapsed in a heap on the hard stone floor. As she watched her brother lying motionless on the floor, Lavinia struggled and writhed and finally freed herself of the ropes at her feet and hands.

Lavinia ran toward her brother and managed to pull him through the cage of stone pillars. Still breathing. She looked around the room, thinking about what to do next. She needed to get them out of this place, get them somewhere safe. Just then, four Bargouls poured through the doorway into the room. They did not speak but moved toward Lavinia and grabbed her. She struggled, kicking and punching, even managing to connect with some of her attackers, but there were too many of them. The Bargouls carried Lavinia out of the room and back into the chamber with the tear. Lavinia screamed when she realized what they planned to do. With a large heave, the Bargouls tossed Lavinia into the undulating tear as her screams echoed through the room.

As soon as Mya entered the tear, the pain stopped. She opened her eyes. She was in a small chapel; wooden benches and meager candles were the only decorations. At the front was an altar with a body spread upon it. She approached.

"Hey," said the person lying on the altar.

"No," said Mya, realizing who it was. "No, it can't be."

Mya's eyes moved slowly over her half-brother; this boy she had grown so close to and with him had gone through so much. He looked slight and tired, in some ways peaceful, but something about him struck Mya; her mind refusing to accept the reality before her.

"Michael, I . . ." she did not have the words. She thought about the struggle and the fights, the battles and the tragedies, their mother, both their fathers; lost; so much lost and now him too. She refused to accept it.

"Mya, don't cry," said Michael, raising his upper body from the altar and leaning back on his elbows. He watched Mya's bright eyes fill with tears and one of them slowly trickled down her cheek.

"I don't want to lose you. You gave me so much," she pleaded. Michael offered her his hand, such a simple gesture. She placed her's inside.

"It's okay Mya. This place . . ." said Michael, looking around the dimly lit chapel. "You made this place for me."

"I don't understand."

"It's alright. You have grown so much Mya and I only wish I could have been with you more; I'm sorry for leaving for all that time . . ." he trailed off as though pondering this last word.

"I forgive you Michael." She tightened her hand around Michael's.

"Look over there," said Michael, pointing. Mya followed the trail of his hand and saw a glowing doorway, oval shaped and lined with light. "Allcraft is through there. You can still stop him."

"Is there enough time?" said Mya, not wanting to leave her brother's side.

"There is always enough time, Mya. The Twinning is even more powerful than either of us know. Look there," said Michael, pointing in another direction. Mya looked and saw another door, just like the first, glowing in the shadows. "The Twinning controls it all Mya; Earth, Serafina, nature . . . even time. Do you remember my father's Departure?"

Mya started, surprised by the question. She had not thought about Peter's Departure in a very long time; ever since her mother got sick; now her mind returned to that day and she told Michael the whole story. He listened intently from his resting place on the glowing altar. Mya told her brother everything she rememberd; her memory from Peter Smith's departure, about the Orators and how her mother looked in that white gown. "Does this make sense to you at all?"

"Yes Mya. Thank you for telling me that story," he said, smiling. "And our mother grew sick just after the Departure, right? There is more to be seen at the Departure than you remember, our mother saw to that. She saved that moment for you, for right now Mya."

Mya never made the connection before but he was right; it was shortly after the Departure she started to see the first signs of the illness.

"You should go there," said Michael. "Use the door. It should be ready for you now."

"How do you know all of this Michael?"

"Allcraft showed me a great deal when I was with him but his anger and jealously always kept him at bay. He could never control the Twinning because he let his greed control him. You are nothing like him Mya. You are the one." Now Mya realized why her brother looked and felt so strange; he was softly glowing and she could see it just around the corners of his eyes.

Mya glanced at the second door Michael pointed to and thought about what he just said. "You mean . . . I can go back?"

"The Twinning is like an ocean Mya; just as it would be impossible to change the ocean's current you cannot influence the Twinning's flow but you can sail upon its waves and go where you choose."

"Where I choose . . ." she looked again at the door.

"Mya, this place . . . is special. You have all the time you need but you don't have everything you will need to defeat him. Only you can find it." Michael smiled, bright and long, the way Mya always remembered him in her head; the boy in her rose field.

"You can do this Mya. It is up to you now. I cannot help you anymore. It has always been you Mya. You are a Seraphim now and the world will heed to your will. Stop him Mya. Stop him and find me again . . . someday."

Mya could not control the tears now; they streamed down her face like raindrops on flower petals. Michael lay back down on the altar and closed his eyes. Mya watched him lying there, peaceful; like he was asleep. His long, dark hair lay in tangled messes around his face but still his eyes seemed to glow with subtle, white light. Mya let go of his hand and gently placed it at her brother's side upon the altar. For several moments she waited, her eyes brimming with tears, but the moment did not last long; she would not allow herself the gift of grief now, not when so much remained unfinished. She glanced around the small chapel. One door led to Allcraft and the other . . .

Mya approached the second door. A door through time? Mya did not know. She could see no handle or knob of any kind. She approached slowly; one step, two and then, silently she vanished into a soft, white light.

CHAPTER 29

▼

THE DEPARTURE

Moving from the darkness of the chapel, the light from the cliffside momentarily blinded Mya. She stood far back from the others, standing on a hillside overlooking the people gathered to say goodbye to Peter Smith. She could see her mother, Lillian; her long, white gown whipping in the soft sea-breeze. Next to her Mya observed the Mayweather family, shaking hands with someone and nodding their heads. She saw an Orator standing near a large casket, his Departure Robes flowing in the same breeze as Lillian's dress. Lucious and Lavinia rested near the others, seated under a large tree enjoying the shade. As Mya watched from the hillside, she saw Dunny and Quixitix saunter over to her mother and a feeling of deep regret spread through her, a longing to see her friends once more. Then she saw herself.

There she was, Mya VanVargott, standing by her mother's side. She looked at her own long, dirty blonde hair. Not quite as long as it fell now. She watched herself embrace her mother; bury her own head into Lillian's comforting arms. Her expression was clear even from the hillside on which she observed herself; deep remorse. She watched all the people she knew so well move about, speak with each other. A few of them glanced up to the hillside but she did not think they recognized her.

She glanced to her left and caught a brief glimpse of a dark figure hidden behind a tree. Michael. She did not have much time to react to Michael's presence. When she returned her gaze to the Departure she saw something unbelievable and something she certainly had no memory of. Everyone at the departure simply dropped to the ground, fell into heaps all at the same time.

Everyone except Lillian. Mya watched as Lillian remained standing, motionless for a few moments, her head up to the sky. Mya did not move either, a silent observer of this most important of events.

From her robes, Lillian produced a book. Mya knew which book it was. Placing her hand on the front, Lillian closed her eyes. The book glowed, very brightly, and Mya watched as streams of light seemed to flow from the tome, moving through the air and fluttering off like stray birds. Lillian placed the book on the ground and from her robes produced another one. Again she placed her hands on the cover and this time the fluttering light moved into the book, culled from the air. Mya watched in amazement at what Lillian did, her power so pure and great. When she was done, Lillian held the second book up into the air and turned toward Mya. Mya, unsure if her mother could even see her, remained motionless. She watched her mother speak and Mya could not understand how she was able to hear the words.

"This is for you Mya. Only you can use it. This is my gift to you. The power of the Seraphim. The voice of the Twinning, for you to sing. If you sing it, there is nothing you cannot do. I love you Mya."

Then, Mya heard a sweet singing, a voice so delicate and pure Mya could do nothing but surrender to it. It was her mother singing but not just her mother. It was the

Seraphim, ringing through the air as all who were gathered slept around them. Lillian had created this moment in time, this secret ceremony meant only for Mya, with the last of her life and will. Mya listened to the song and let it wash through her, fill her up, and when it ended, the people were standing again as if nothing had happened, listening to an Orator speak about the life of Peter Smith. Mya looked around and did not see Michael. She closed her eyes and the scene vanished. Mya found herself once more inside the chapel. She felt different somehow. She did not approach the altar this time but instead made her way to the other door. She brushed the hair from her face, clutched the book in her hands and walked through.

CHAPTER 30

▼

THE SONG OF THE SERAPHIM

Three figures stood silhouetted against the dark blue sky of Earth. Lucas Allcraft, his black coat swaying in the breeze along with his onyx hair. Next to Lucas stood Lavinia Allcraft; Fabricantress and descendant of Lucas Allcraft, held tight against her will. Rounding out the trio was Bartlebug, the loyal and sinister servant of the most infamous Magican to ever live.

"I've come to end this Allcraft," said Mya, shouting against the wind. The dark hillside upon which they stood trembled in the gusts.

"Too late," he said, his back still turned to her. Mya watched as Allcraft grabbed the back of Lavinia's neck and thrust her forward. In his other hand he held his red Culling Stone, home to all the voices of the now silenced Seraphim, channeling the power of the Twinning through him and into Lavinia. In the distance, a mountain crumbled; Mya felt the Earth tremble even at this distance. In its place a massive volcano rose and when it reached its apex, began to spew red lava. The sky darkened and turned grey. The wind grew cold.

Without turning around, Allcraft summoned the Magicant and sent a flash of fiery rocks hurtling toward Mya. Without flinching, the Fabricant came to her aid and

246

shielded her from the bevy, the twin forces cancelling each other out.

"Don't bother Fabricantress," said Allcraft, turning and looking at her over his shoulder. "It's already done. This world is gone, it is ash. I have already begun remaking it."

"That doesn't mean I can't undo it," said Mya, her voice unwavering, determined, and dark.

Allcraft said nothing, turning to face Mya. She saw the Culling Stone fully now, its red glow unmistakable and pulsing with power. Lavinia's face, a terrified mix of emotion, begged Mya for help, and Bartlebug stood ready, his eyes deadly white and his stinger exposed.

"Then I suppose we are at an impasse," said Allcraft, smiling.

"No," said Mya, confident and sure. "Because I have this."

From her waist Mya produced the book; The Song of the Seraphim; the ancient text imbued with the very power and essence of the Seraphim. "And because your dark soul can never stand up to the light of the Seraphim."

The book began to emit a holy light, glowing and pure, and then the light shot forward, striking Bartlebug before he could react. The jolt sent the Bargoul reeling backward and he cried out as he fell back over the edge of the cliff, barely able to hang on against the thrashing wind. He screamed loudly, his voice a shriek as the wind took him reeling over the edge.

"Lavinia, you can come here now," said Mya. Lavinia looked at Allcraft, his hand still tight around her collar, but Allcraft did not move. Again the book shot a blast of light, this time at the hand holding Lavinia back. Allcraft screamed and was forced to release her. In that moment Lavinia ran toward Mya and stood by her side, protected by the book.

"No!" shouted Allcraft. "I will not be defeated again by the Fabricant, by the half-witted, weaker side of the Twinning. The Magicant shall prevail!" He screamed, enraged, and again summoned the Magicant, throwing all the might of his fury and power at Mya. She simply stood still and the Shield of the Seraphim appeared, protecting her, Lavinia and the book from anything Allcraft could do. His scream filled the landscape as he brought down burning fire from above, massive rock clusters and icy, frozen blades. Mya just stood calmly beneath the soft glow of the Shield. Finally, Allcraft abandoned his assault. Breathless, he spoke.

"Everyone you love is dead, girl. Why not give up? What hope do you have?"

Mya smiled. "There is always hope, Lucas. Even in the deepest darkness, even in the most dire times, hope remains." Mya closed the book and the light it gave off faded. She handed the book to Lavinia and approached Allcraft; on the cliffside they looked like polar opposites; Mya in white and Allcraft in black, two sides of one ever spinning coin. She stared at him, the Magican responsible for so much pain and strife, the man who had haunted her dreams for so long and brought her world to its end. Allcraft stared back into the eyes of a woman he both hated and feared, a power he never really understood yet always longed for. The wind whipped their clothes around them in swirling eddies and the sound of destruction rained down all around them. Mya could smell the ash from the burning world around her and Allcraft could hear the screams of the Earth tearing itself apart.

"It's over," said Mya, reaching out her hand. She looked at the Culling Stone.

Allcraft stood, speechless and unable to move or react.

"No. I have defeated kings and I have bested the Order! I have waited hundreds of years for this moment and I will not be denied!"

Before Mya could react, Allcraft shot his hand toward her and grabbed her by the hair. Mya, caught off guard, could not react quickly enough and suddenly she knew what Allcraft was doing. His teeth seemed to glow in the dark night as he sneered at her, his lips curling into a serpentine smile.

Lavinia watched Allcraft grab Mya and reel backwards, toward the cliff. Lavinia gasped as Allcraft screamed out and, with Mya in his grip, threw himself from the top of the cliff. Lavinia ran forward as fast as she could, sliding on her knees toward the edge, hoping she would find Mya hanging on. Instead, all she saw when she looked down was two figures, falling fast, clutching one another as if in an embrace, plummeting toward the jagged and jutting rocks below. She watched them fall and then noticed the light begin to change; everything grew darker. She looked around at the world, shocked and terrified; it was going out. The world was going out. The moonlight faded and darkness crept in from the horizon, unnaturally fast like ink pouring from a well. Lavinia watched as the light around her grew smaller and smaller, as the world, as Earth simply ceased to exist, with no Song to create it, it simply faded away like a dying flame, put out by the tireless machinations of Lucas Allcraft. They were too late; he had won. She began to cry, a single tear, and a small intake of breath, and then she too was gone.

Only empty darkness remained.

"Hey again," said Mya. She stood above her brother, Michael, as he lay on the altar in the chapel.

"You came back."

"Yea," said Mya. "It's over. I stopped him."

"I'm glad," said Michael, smiling. "What now?"

"I have an idea, but you're not going to like it."

Michael frowned. "I already know what it is. Are you ready?"

"I am. It took me a while to figure it all out, but this was my calling all along. This is what the Seraphim wanted from me." Michael nodded.

"Here is what I wanted to give you." From his pocket Michael pulled a single, red rose and handed it to Mya. She ran her fingers along the stem. The stem felt smooth and contained no thorns, nothing to harm her.

"From my field?" she asked. He nodded and smiled.

"You should start there," he said.

"I think I will."

"Mya?" said Michael as his sister turned away from him.

"There is always hope. Hope never ends. Life never ends. Just remember that. It is all connected, in the end."

Mya smiled. "Thank you Michael. Goodbye."

"Goodbye Mya."

Michael nodded and Mya walked back toward the door of the chapel. She opened it and entered into darkness.

It was all around her; the world just an empty, dark place. It was a strange feeling to be surrounded by nothingness. Everything was gone and only she remained. She looked at the rose, smelled it. The aroma was just as she remembered. She closed her eyes and smiled and then a small, white light rose from her lips. She felt light and she felt good; whole. The world was gone . . . faded to darkness . . . to emptiness and for a moment, just one fleeting moment, Mya was gone too. Then a voice from the darkness . . . a sacred Word followed by many more . . . and a song . . .

And then . . .

light Wrist
level
resounding
growth
caress Street
basket paper
Book Mud
magnum madre
twines
material
glass overzealous
Adam mystical
Night
chart
scintillating
scrape
pumpkin
California equality
Twilight onion
Ring
underground
actress Piano
righteous
Shirt
love
bright
joystick
Forest beach opine
meaning
seventeen

Epilogue

Michael Smith blinked once, then twice, then opened his eyes. The room was quiet and peaceful, no sounds really, except the occasional chirp of a bird. He inhaled deeply. Swinging his legs over the side of the bed he stood and saw the rose, bright red and alive, resting on his nightstand. He smiled. She really was everywhere around them, in everything. He glanced around the room and his eyes lighted upon his bookcase; filled, shelf to shelf, with his favorites. He could almost hear the waves lapping aginst the side of that pirate ship from *Treasure Island*. His eyes stopped for a moment on one book in particular; one very special book resting upon his shelf. It would always be safe there. He smiled.

"Up already?" the voice, adult and masculine, greeted Michael.

"Yea Dad," he said.

"Good. Dunny and Quixitix are already at the table," laughed Mr. Smith. "Your mother should be home soon, too."

"That's good," said Michael. He picked up the rose and looked out the window of his room. He saw Lucious and Lavinia there, just sitting together on an old tree stump, talking; the sun on their backs, rising as it once had and rising as it will again. In the distance, mountains stretched to the horizon and a few wispy, strolling clouds lingered in the deep blue sky; a sky so blue it reminded Michael of one he once gazed upon, a lifetime ago. He could feel his sister everywhere around him.

He watched Lucious and Lavinia playing in the field outside and imagined their lives from this point on. Imagined the world they would help to create, the world into which they would place their hope. Michael looked down at his feet for a moment, thinking, feeling the rise and fall of his own chest, the steady inhale and exhale of his own breath. Everything connected.

He looked back out the window at the twins, listened to their laughter as they enjoyed the warm sun and all around them, spreading for miles in every direction, as far as Michael could see; red roses, soft and without thorns.

Just the way Mya made them.

The End

Author's Note

Without the love, support and constant interest of my friends
and family these books could never have been written.
Thank you so very much.
Thank you also to all the Twinning fans out there who
contributed words to the final chapter. You made this a
reality for me.

Erica C.   **Autumn F. K.**
Erin S.   **Chi N.**
Krystin C. O.   **Adrianne H.**
Laura B. S.   **Kim H. C.**
Steve S.   **Martina R.**
Joli B. M.
John C.
Jared C.
Jordan C.
Carol C.
Mara K. T.
Matt T.

The journey is what you make it.
Fondest regards,
Justin R. Cary